HOT DADDIES

HOT DADDIES

GAY EROTIC FICTION

Edited by
Richard Labonté

CLEiS
PRESS

Published in the United States by Cleis Press Inc., 2246 Sixth Street, Berkeley, California 94710.

Printed in the United States.
Cover design: Scott Idleman/Blink
Cover photograph: Glen Mitchell
Text design: Frank Wiedemann
First Edition.
10 9 8 7 6 5 4 3 2 1

Trade paper ISBN: 978-1-57344-712-6
E-book ISBN: 978-1-57344-735-5

For Asa:
twenty years on,
gray becomes him

Contents

INTRODUCTION

Sometimes an older man is a father figure, a replacement Dad, mentoring a younger man's self-acceptance, proffering wisdom, serving as a role model for the queer world.

Sometimes an older man is a Daddy, demanding a mix of sexual indoctrination and physical domination, training a younger man—a boy, a son, a boi—in the ways of the S/M community, and serving, again, as a role model for a subset of the queer world.

Both gay archetypes, of older seducing/indoctrinating/succoring younger, figure in this collection. But there are age-reversal variations on the standard theme, too, as there are in real life. In Landon Dixon's arch "Men of the Open Road," a young hitchhiker knows where he wants to go with older men—and it's not farther down the road. The younger man has the power to seduce—and to instruct—in Randy Turk's powerful "Professor Papi"; and, again, older is set free by younger in Jamie Freeman's elegant "In His Time."

And, in a variation on a variation, there is Dale Chase's

introspective "Never Say Never Again," in which a middle-aged man, nurtured by a dead Daddy, seeks renewal in relationships with younger men.

In other stories, "fathers" figure more centrally than—but certainly as erotically as—Daddies: Dominic Santi's epistolary "Settling In: Letter to Jack" offers an older man's exasperation with his younger partner's antics; Mark Wildyr's haunting "Markey" is about a boy's hero-worship for the older brother he never had; Gavin Atlas's on-the-lam "Daddies in Damian" is all about rescuing the lad; David Holly's liberating "Pop Tingle" is another rescue fable—about saving a boy from the streets to let him realize his potential; and Jack Fritscher's muscular "Father and Son Tag Team (That Summer! That Camp! That Cousin!)," is a no-hole-barred sexual romp with a summer camp counselor reveling in an older man's mature power and a younger man's fresh appeal.

Then there are the hardcore (but always erotically playful) Daddy stories by Xan West, Doug Harrison, Kyle Lukoff, and Jeff Mann, two of them younger authors, two of them veterans of the topic, all of them capturing with been-there verisimilitude the Daddy-son dynamics of dominance and submission, toughness and tenderness, teaching and learning—a genre in gay erotic fiction, a truth in real life.

All of the stories in *Hot Daddies* are about men in relationships. That wasn't the intention. But anthologies, within the boundaries of good storytelling, good writing and an editor's acumen and taste take on a life of their own. No one-night encounters here, then—the Daddies and the sons are in it for the long haul.

Richard Labonté
Bowen Island, British Columbia

IN HIS TIME

Jamie Freeman

The chandelier in the foyer was still swinging in the wake of Penny's furious departure when Steve decided to go to the bookstore. He looked down at his hands, still shaking from the fight-induced adrenaline, and mentally counted back in time. *How long had it been? Four years? No, longer than that. Had it been five?*

He sat on the sofa, letting the urgency build until it propelled him in the direction of his shoes. He slipped his feet into his Nikes and walked over to the hall mirror. He was lean from running, but his severe eyes and close-cropped, conservative beard played tricks on his eyes. Most of the time he liked the beard, thought it made him look roguish and rebellious, but tonight when he looked into the scratched antique glass, his father's stern visage stared back at him.

He considered going upstairs to shave; he considered kicking his Nikes back into the closet, maybe sinking into a whiskey sour and watching the Rays with his feet up on the coffee table.

Indecision made him shift from his right foot to his left.

Five goddamn years. It had been five, not four.

He pushed his left toe against the back of his right shoe, testing his resolve.

He glanced back into the mirror; a blond forelock dropped in front of his steely blue eyes and his father was gone. His face was handsome and still, timeless as the frozen photograph of an aging movie star.

He blinked.

Go, go, go. Just go.

He hurried out to his car.

As he backed his old Mercedes out of the driveway, he waved to Mrs. Alexander, who was pruning the azalea bushes that separated their yards. She waved back, flashing an inquisitive smile that made Steve snarl with annoyance. Her pursed lips and tightly knitted brow told him she was making note of his rapid departure. She glanced at her watch and her smile grew broader. He grimaced, knew she would hold this little nugget of information close, clutching it to her venomous breast until she could release it into the credulous hands of his wife, perhaps over iced tea or lemonade or homemade lemon squares, served on her verandah under ceiling fans that stirred hot air redolent with smiles and floral perfume and pettiness.

And Penny would accept the proffered clue like she had accepted all the others, goaded by the old woman's cool, papery whisper, to construct an angry, fractious narrative that cast Steve as the adulterous villain. "Maybe he's involved with that pretty colored girl who works for him," she'd whisper. "You know a man doesn't keep himself looking that fine for the woman he marries." And Penny would sit on Mrs. Alexander's porch for hours, rocking in the straight-backed rocker, with a hard, empty look in her eyes.

But Steve had stopped everything when they'd married, stopped the cruising and the meet-ups, stopped the men on the side, and it had been five years since he'd done more than look. So he was condemned for keeping himself in shape; for plodding through year after year in an unhappy marriage; for keeping his marriage vow despite the desire that threatened to engulf him.

Tonight when she got back from her tantrum, Penny would turn to the old woman for hand-patting pity, offered with barely concealed relish, and they would scowl at him from their rockers. Penny would stop talking to him and lock him out of his own bedroom. And he would fall asleep in the study in front of the television watching old reruns of "Will & Grace" and feeling sorry for himself.

Five goddamn years.

Just go, Steve.

His eyes were hot and wet as he turned the corner, leaving Mrs. Alexander behind, opening the sunroof and flooring the accelerator.

Dusk was settling over the town and the streets were waking sporadically, neon signs flickering to life here and there while others remained dark in the overheated half-light. Steve turned up the air-conditioning and rubbed his hands across his bare thighs, his stomach tightening as he turned onto Vanderbilt. He pulled in behind the store and parked close to the building, pulling his car in tightly between an old Volvo and a Jeep.

He took a deep breath, ran his fingers through his hair and looked in the flip-down visor mirror, trying to remember what it had been like to be beautiful and young. Time had passed so quickly. He barely recognized the image in the mirror. The sharpness had diffused from his once-angular features. His face had filled out, becoming rounder and less precise, like a stone worn smooth by a waterfall. The vision of his father peering out from beneath his close-cropped beard in the hall mirror had ruined the look for him forever; he would shave when he got home. And his eyes: when had they started to sag around the edges, their color fading from glowing sapphire to steely blue-gray?

Fuck it. He knew he was still attractive, even if the comments were qualified now, as if his attractiveness, once a broad and ungovernable thing, had been corralled by time, confined to the back pasture with the goats and the geldings. He'd heard people say it behind his back. "Great for his age," they said, and "hardly looks like he's in his forties." He'd turned forty in May, for Christ's sake. True, he'd heard "hot for his age" once, from Wendy, the grad student who was sleeping with his department chair, and he'd tried to take the comments as compliments, but they dug at him like a dozen rose thorns embedded in his palms. He cringed when they said it, especially the interns and the newest crop of MBAs with their expensive cars, family money, and wind-blown, male-model faces.

And then yesterday, as he'd rounded the corner and walked into the conference room, he'd heard Kevin's lush tenor voice saying, "I'd be all up in that daddy's business if he—" Steve looked up into the startled, blushing faces of Kevin, Aya and the Indian kid whose name he didn't know. The four of them stood in a silent standoff for an awkward moment before Aya and the Indian kid made some excuse to slink from the room. Kevin laid a hand on Steve's arm and started to say something, but other people arrived for the meeting and the moment was washed away in a sea of agendas and budgets and spreadsheets.

Steve brooded through the meeting, his eyebrows knitted over dark, stormy eyes.

He'd heard the compliment in the word; seen the lascivious fire dancing in Kevin's eyes; felt the heat of his fingertips. But the narrative shift bothered him. He had been a beautiful boy and he had prided himself on the ease with which he had carried that beauty through his twenties and thirties. He'd always traded on his looks for whatever he wanted, including favors from dozens of men over the years; dozens of furtive, cruisy encounters in bathrooms and parks and gym showers, or nameless blow-and-go's arranged online.

Daddy? Really? Five goddamn years out of the game and suddenly the rules shift? What the fuck?

He shook his head and slid the cover across the visor mirror. He would not think about this now. It was pointless to dwell on the shift while the clock was ticking. Penny would be home by nine, so he had less than two hours to make something happen.

He broke a sweat in the ten yards to the door of the bookstore.

He tugged on the door, the bells mounted on the inside jangling to announce his arrival. A dozen pairs of eyes flicked in his direction, some dropping away, others watching with interest as he hopped down the four steps to the main floor.

He knew his calves looked good coming down the steps; he allowed himself a little grin and felt better about his prospects.

Steve did a quick survey of the room: two young ones laughing and vamping beside the movie magazines; an old guy over by the adult magazines; five—no, six muscled, cotton-clad jocks; a pair of gawky med students drinking coffee and leaning close over a small café table in the front window; three or four boys barely out of high school; a pretty, waifish emo in an Edward Gorey T-shirt; a peppering of older guys reading *Martha Stewart Living* or *Cat Fancy* or John Sandford. He circled for a moment, glanced at his watch, and then noticed a dark-haired young man intently reading a paperback mystery. He stood with his right foot resting on his left, balanced in an absent, improbable stance, absorbed in the words on the page in front of him. He seemed oblivious to the attention that eddied around him, oblivious to his own disheveled beauty. Steve stopped and stared appraisingly at the boy's long, muscular body, pale skin, and lustrous hair. The boy looked up as he turned a page, dark eyes focusing for a moment on Steve. He looked startled and then he smiled. Steve was suddenly uncharacteristically bashful, looking down pathetically at the shelves in front of him, picking up a biography of Idi Amin and feigning interest in the grainy cover photo. He flipped the book over, catching a glimpse of the boy, who was still watching Steve with a look that was both sly and serene. Steve pantomimed an interest in the back cover of the book in his hands, running his eyes pointlessly across the rows of letters and spaces. His mouth dried up like a summer lakebed.

Normally Steve liked this moment: the moment of discovery, the moment he stepped into a secluded clearing to confront a dappled deer. In that moment he was neither predator nor prey. He was one of two beasts sniffing the wind to confirm the possibility of desire. Sometimes the richness of the moment led to something heart-racingly crazy. And sometimes the moment passed unnoticed by the deer, and Steve moved on.

Tonight Steve was edgy, clumsy from lack of practice. Damp leaves brushed against his cheeks as he raised his head from the book in his hands and stepped into the clearing, locking eyes with the boy. Steve's desire rested at the still point of the pursuit, waiting patiently for the next thing to happen, waiting for the moment of recognition or dismissal.

But the boy gave neither.

They stood frozen in place.

The room stirred around them; men shifting, pacing and watching.

And the boy dropped his eyes back to his book, dark eyebrows furrowed in concentration, turning the page with long, pale fingers.

Steve felt weightless and disoriented.

One of the others stepped into their clearing. A middle-aged man in baggy running shorts and a T-shirt walked down the aisle toward the dark-haired beauty, and then stopped next to him, kneeling to tie and retie his shoe, glancing pointedly, questioningly at the boy's crotch. The boy remained frozen, his eyes roving from side to side down the page of the novel in his hands. The predator rose to his feet, brushed past the boy, closer than he needed to, and ambled back toward the café. Steve watched him go and then turned back to the boy, who smiled, just the barest twitch of muscle beneath pale skin, but Steve saw it and his pulse beat faster in response.

Steve heard a nervous cough behind him. He turned slowly, swiveling to find himself confronted by the coolly expectant eyes of a balding man in brown slacks. The old man waggled his wooly eyebrows and flicked his eyes downward. Steve looked at the man's hands: shoved deep in the pockets of his pants, they stretched the fabric tight over a long, thin erection. Steve looked up into the man's pale, muddy eyes and raised his right eyebrow.

The aging predator misread the signal and took a step closer to Steve. He reached out and brushed his bare knuckles along Steve's muscular thigh, his breathing growing heavier.

Steve shifted his weight away and whispered, "Beat it, man."

How close am I to this? Steve fingers trembled.

He turned back to look at the boy, who still held the book in his hands, but who had been watching Steve's interaction with curious attention.

Steve winked. The boy grinned, shrugged—*What're ya*

gonna do?—and looked back down at his book.

Steve watched him without pretense now. He let his eyes move slowly across the even, bluish stubble that played across the boy's jawline and upped his initial age estimate to twenty, maybe twenty-one. A permanent blush splashed across the boy's cheeks, rising like the crest of a wave over the fine line of his jaw. His hair curled uncontrollably in broad waves that lapped gently against the back of his neck.

Steve watched the soft cotton of the boy's shirt rising and falling with the steady rhythm of his breathing. There were thick muscled planes beneath the cotton, nipples that strained ever so slightly against cool restraint and a few silky chestnut hairs that crested the collar. The boy's arms were smooth marble beneath a carpet of lightly curling hair that tapered as it approached his finely crafted hands. He had perfectly proportioned fingers, firm but delicate with closely clipped nails, and he wore a thick silver band with a pattern of interlocking circles.

Steve's cock stirred inside his running shorts. He wished now he had worn underwear. His shirt hid his excitement for the moment, but he knew that by folding his hands across his chest, he could lift his shirt just enough to reveal his considerable assets. Although he had counted on a carefully orchestrated curtain call to finalize the delicate negotiations, now he felt self-conscious, fearing everyone in the store was aware of his growing erection. The image of the old predator's brown slacks stretched across his long, thin erection flashed through Steve's mind.

How close am I to becoming that? That guy is what? Ten years older than me? And I'm what? Twenty years older than this boy?

His hands started to tremble again. He reached out to pick up a book, hoping the solidity of the volume in his hand would somehow ground him.

Fuck that. I'm nothing like that guy.

"Excuse me, sir," a voice said from behind him.

Steve turned aside to make room as a tall, handsome boy slipped past him and approached his quarry.

"Jason,"

"Oh, hey, Dave. S'up?" Soft lilting tones that rumbled with baritone fire.

Steve moved a few steps closer, picking up a biography of Disraeli and intently reading the first paragraph of the introduction. Over and over he read the lines, the words mingling with the conversation beside him, and the entire soaring jumble presided over by the single sound—*Jason*. Steve's lips moved inadvertently and he looked up just as the two boys turned to look at him. He had spoken the word aloud. "Jason." He blushed and muttered something about Disraeli, turning his gaze back between the pages and wondering if he should just flee into the night. Perhaps he should just go home and beat off in the shower. He set the book down and turned to go.

He walked the length of the aisle but, instead of turning left toward the door, he turned right and walked over to the adult magazines, pushing rather more roughly than he had intended past the man in brown, reaching up to pluck a copy of *Stroke* off the shelf. He felt the blush receding from his cheeks as he blocked the rest of the store out and buried himself in the warm folds of the magazine.

He flipped through the pages. *No, no, no.* He put the magazine back and pulled down another and then another and another. *Nothing. Nothing.* There was nothing there, nothing but skinny legs and vacant, drugged-out stares, or top-heavy, muscled porn gods, round and swollen like man-shaped water balloons.

He tossed the magazine back toward the shelves. It fluttered and flapped, falling and dragging half a dozen others to the floor. Faces turned in his direction and he felt his cheeks burning.

He leaned over to pick up the magazines, glancing back at Jason as he gathered the mess.

Steve could see the outline of the boy's ass beneath the worn denim, round and perfect. He imagined grasping the damp cloth just below the small of Jason's back and peeling it down over the ripe, round mounds. There would be heat and the sweetly acrid smell of sweat and Steve would drop to his knees and slide his hands along the twin mounds, fuzzy as peaches and taut under his palms. He would slide his fingertips close, delving into the crevice and then pulling the cheeks apart to reveal—

Fingers brushed along Steve's arm as a man in tight jeans and a wifebeater pushed past him. Their eyes met and a beat of recognition passed between them. Steve saw the inside of a gas station restroom, a muscular form bent over the filthy toilet, Steve's fingers curled through damp, dirty-blond hair, Steve fucking and grunting and coming into a pale blue condom. It was a flash of memory, like an image glimpsed from a speeding car window, and then the man was moving away, sauntering to the end of the aisle before turning and looking at Steve with a somber, acne-scarred face that looked at least a decade older than the one Steve remembered.

Steve tried to lick his lips, but his mouth was too dry.

His erection was throbbing painfully now. He was so parched and so choked with need he was having trouble swallowing. Need was now a physical force, swelling inside him, filtering up from his stomach and slicing like a deadly knife blade through the nipples that strained visibly beneath his tight shirt.

Sweat trickled down his back; the overhead fluorescents burned like halogens. He turned back toward Jason and this time their eyes met and held. Jason had been watching him, interest finally playing across his previously placid face. His eyebrow cocked and Steve gave him a half nod in response.

Jason turned to go and Steve slipped down the aisle to the back of the store. He heard the bells and then rounded the corner to see Jason pushing the back door outward. The boy glanced back once and then vanished into the humid night.

Outside in the darkness, Steve regained his composure.

He approached the boy and they talked for a few minutes about the heat and how quiet the campus was during the summer.

"I'm Steve, by the way."

"Jason—"

"—I know."

"—Oh, right."

They stumbled over each other and then Jason laughed nervously.

"That was kinda creepy, you saying my name like that. It was like you were praying," he said.

"Well, I was...um, I dunno, being stupid, I guess."

"Not very articulate for a guy who's reading a Disraeli biography."

"No. No, you're right. I guess I was just distracted."

"Were you, now?"

"I was, indeed."

Jason grinned, stepped back and leaned against the back of an old, boxy Volvo. His T-shirt rode up revealing a trail of crisp dark curls that rose from beneath the low-slung waistband of his jeans.

"Nice," Steve said.

"It gets even better." Jason's voice was soft but deep, pitched to his audience with the precision of a stage actor.

"I bet it does."

There was a long pause.

"I believe it's your serve," Jason said.

"I want to fuck you," Steve said.

"Well, that kind of serve'll win you the game every time, Steve."

Steve's office was old but large, with bookshelves, leather chairs, and a worn leather sofa that faced a huge antique desk. Jason looked around, switched on a Tiffany lamp on a side table and picked up a framed photo of Penny.

"Married?" he asked.

"Separated," Steve said.

"She's beautiful."

"Yes." Steve stood next to the edge of his desk watching the boy like a man who had invited a gazelle into his living room.

"You're not separated," Jason said, stepping closer to Steve.

"No."

"But you're unhappy."

"Yes."

"And yet you stay."

"A guy makes a vow," Steve said, looking away.

"A guy's got a good heart," Jason said.

Steve turned back and looked at him in silence; the hair on his arms stood on end.

"What?" he asked.

"Nothing. Sorry. I'm always bringing down the mood of the room," Jason said. He touched Steve's cheek, turning his face gently so that their eyes met again. "We don't have to talk about the outside."

Steve swallowed audibly and then blushed under the intensity of Jason's silent gaze.

"I sound calm when I'm nervous. It's annoying," Jason said.

Steve let out a short snort of laughter.

Jason let his hand drop from Steve's face and walked over to the sofa. He dropped onto the seat, sitting back with his arms draped along the tops of the cushions. His legs were spread wide at the knees with a nonchalance that brought Steve's cock back to attention.

He could see the outline of Jason's cock growing beneath the denim.

"How old are you, Jason?"

"Why?" He grinned. "You worried?"

"No, no. It's not that, it's just that..."

"I'm twenty-three."

"Grad student?"

"MFA."

"Theater?"

"Writing."

"Oh."

"Yeah, that's what my dad said when I told him."

"You seem older," Steve said.

"You're a charmer, Stevarino."

"Preternaturally calm, insightful, articulate—"

"Trying to make up points now?"

"—beautiful."

"Beautiful?" Jason looked embarrassed for the first time since they'd met.

"Beautiful."

"I guess I don't think of myself that way—"

"Oh, come on, Jason."

"No, really. Beautiful doesn't really resonate with me."

"I find that hard to believe."

Jason shrugged. "It's more about attitude. I like a big, rugged older man: someone whose soul has a little heft; someone whose body has some thickness to it; someone who knows what he's doing; someone who's not afraid of himself." There was a challenge in his eyes now. "Is that you, Steve?"

"That's me."

"So what're you gonna do to me, Steve?"

"I'm gonna make you scream so loud, the security officers from the next building are gonna come running in here with their guns in their hands."

"I like the sound of that." Jason leaned back and rubbed his cock through his jeans.

Steve slipped off his running shoes and discarded his socks.

"Keep rubbing yourself," Steve said.

The boy's hand moved and his breathing became louder.

Steve dropped to his knees between Jason's spread legs, taking Jason's feet in his hands and easing off each of the loafers with a gentle tug. His hands explored the warm muscles of the boy's feet, massaging the soles through the soft cotton. He peeled back the socks and held his left foot in his hands, running his fingers lightly along the instep, fingering the hair that curled along the bridge and delicately punctuated the toes. Jason leaned back into the cushions and let his arms fall loose at his sides.

Steve inhaled the exotic fragrance of Jason's sweat, touching the tip of his tongue to the soft underside of the boy's toes. Jason looked up in surprise, his foot jerking involuntarily. He laughed, whispered, "Ticklish," and melted back into the cushions. Steve licked along the length of the boy's sole, memorizing the ridged contours and the tangy taste of him.

Jason moaned softly, turning his head from side to side, but keeping his eyes closed.

Steve sat back on his heels, hearing the crackling pops in his joints as he stood.

Jason looked up at him with soft, curious eyes. His hand rubbed lazily along the length of his cock, tracing the contours through the denim as he watched Steve.

Steve reached down and grabbed the hem of his T-shirt, peeling it up across his firm belly and muscular chest and pulling it over his head. He tossed the shirt at Jason, who let it land with a muffled slap on his face. He inhaled deeply, groaning before he pulled the shirt from his eyes.

Steve stood in front of him in his loose cotton running shorts, tented by his rearing erection. Jason's eyes scanned Steve from head to foot, taking him in with growing excitement. Steve let his own hands caress his chest, brushing his nipples and drawing Jason's eyes to the marbled perfection of his forearms, his collarbone and his flat stomach. He rubbed the head of his cock through the soft cotton of his running shorts, which were damp now with sweat and precum.

"Come here, boy," Steve said.

Jason sat forward on the couch.

"Take it out," Steve said.

Jason reached out and grasped Steve by the hips. He leaned forward to cup his mouth around the hard, cloth-covered cock, blowing a gentle stream of superheated air through the cotton. Steve shuddered and took a half step forward.

Jason's fingers curled around the waistband and slowly pulled Steve's shorts to the floor. He helped Steve step out of them and stood, holding wet cotton to his face, inhaling the musk and moaning again. Steve's cock twitched as he heard the sweat-soaked shorts drop to the floor beside them.

They faced each other, Steve completely naked, Jason barefoot in jeans and T-shirt. Steve looked into his dark eyes and then leaned in fast, kissing him roughly on the lips. Jason stepped into the kiss, pushing the front of his jeans against Steve's cock, letting its damp head slide under the hem of his T-shirt where it finally made fiery contact with his stomach.

Jason reached around to cup Steve's ass, pulling him closer, intensifying the kiss.

Steve reached for Jason's T-shirt, pulling it roughly over his body, exposing the pale expanse of muscle perfectly bisected by a bushy trail of hair that began with the gentle valley between his pecs and descended below the waistband of his jeans. Steve ran his fingers along the furry length of the line, plunging down into the loose jeans, past the elastic of Jason's jockeys to grasp his cock. It was thick and heavy and damp.

"Take off your jeans," Steve said, reaching for the hard twin buds of Jason's nipples and giving them an experimental twist. Jason groaned and squirmed, taking a step back and shoving his jeans and underwear to the floor. He stepped out of them, his long hairy legs finally exposed for Steve's inspection, but before Steve could survey them, the boy threw himself back at Steve, pushing their bodies together and returning to the rough hungry kissing. Steve's face burned under the onslaught of Jason's stubbled face.

Their cocks slid against each other in a confluence of sweat and precum that escalated Jason's excitement. Steve slipped his hand down Jason's back, sliding it lightly across the boy's beautiful ass. He felt the hairs rotating in their follicles, standing at attention under his gentle touch. Jason groaned in appreciation and pushed harder against Steve.

Steve let his hands enjoy the roundness and the downy softness of Jason's ass, lingering in one of the twin dimples before his fingers led him into the warm crevice. His fingertips burned with the wet heat radiating off Jason's skin as his middle fingertip touched the wrinkled pucker of skin that was his destination. He circled the pucker, getting a feel for the small, understated opening before sliding his already damp finger slowly through the muscular ring. Jason gasped, "Oh, god," and then "Oh, god, yes."

Steve pushed his finger farther inside, pushing up against supremely smooth flesh, gauging his progress by the tenor of Jason's groans. He slid his finger back and forth and Jason started to rock, pistoning his body onto Steve's finger.

"Do you want me to fuck you?" Steve whispered.

"Now," Jason said through gritted teeth.

Steve grabbed him roughly by the upper arms and twisted him around to face the sofa, pushing him forward in a kneeling position. Jason leaned forward, bracing himself on the sofa back and pushing his ass backward and upward. Steve grabbed a condom and some lube and stepped up behind the boy. He thought of a joke his father used to tell about Irishmen and boots and stump-trained sheep. He pushed the thought away and rolled the condom on, slapping his cock against his hand to keep it hard. *Really? Right now you're gonna think about your asshole father?* He pushed the thoughts away again, sliding his hand along the crack of Jason's ass, looking at the dark, damp hairs that curled along both sides like exotic vines.

Instead of pushing into the boy, he knelt and pushed his face into the fragrant cleft, letting the smell overwhelm everything else. He licked across Jason's asshole and watched the muscles contract and release.

"Come on, Daddy. Quit knocking and come inside." Jason's voice was low, gravelly with desire. "Fuck me," he said again.

And Steve was on his feet, his hands grasping Jason as he slid his cock in with a single, long stroke. Jason let out a ragged, primordial sound that reverberated up from a wordless place deep inside him. Steve felt the hot internal grip of Jason's body loosening and tightening, showing him the rhythm that would rock them both into oblivion.

He pulled back and slammed all the way in, pushing himself against Jason with the force of a battering ram. Another cry went up from Jason, something that ended in "Oh, god, yeah," and led Steve to a faster, harder rhythm.

Steve pounded Jason's ass, pouring five years of pent-up passion into the boy's clenching body, letting himself disappear into the heat and motion until his mind was gone and his body was ringing like a bell. He grabbed Jason's arms and pulled the boy's body back until his slick back rubbed against Steve's chest. He let his hands explore the elongated muscles of Jason's chest and stomach, groaning in the boy's ear and fucking him harder.

Jason was coaxing him on with his hands, pulling Steve against him, bruising Steve's flesh with his need and taking the full force of his battering. Steve shoved Jason back down onto the sofa. The boy braced himself and moaned. Steve slammed forward like he was trying to cleave Jason in two, and then he could feel himself building to the final crescendo.

"You ready?" he asked.

"I'm ready, Daddy."

Steve picked up the pace, his sweaty feet slipping on the wood floor as he slammed himself home. He wobbled, looked down for a split second to regain his balance and saw a penny on the floor beside his foot. He thought of his wife and faltered.

"Come on, Daddy. Bring it home," Jason groaned.

Steve looked down at the boy's long, muscular back; at his dark, curly hair damp with sweat and felt his power return. He pushed in and out and felt the exquisite strain in his legs, pushing him toward exhaustion. Jason looked over his shoulder and their eyes locked. Jason's pupils were huge, nearly overwhelming the chocolate-brown irises. His eyes were so open and resolute that Steve let them pull him into the next age. He transformed in that instant, taking on a part he had forcefully resisted, transforming irrevocably from youth to middle age, from aging twink to youngish Daddy. He felt strong and hot and alive. He plunged his cock deep into the boy and let out a moan that became a shout, increasing in volume with each wild thrust. And Jason's shout joined his until they were both making a deafening, wordless noise that pushed them past the breathless moment in which they spewed out their seed and collapsed.

And then there was silence.

And then, as they regained themselves, the silence was slowly repopulated by the sounds of their breathing, the ticking of the desk clock, the sounds of the street outside and the hum of the refrigerator in the corner.

They lay in a sweaty tangle on the sofa, Steve crumpled on top of Jason, both of them smeared with cum and lube and trickling sweat. Jason's breathing was slow and rhythmic beneath him, his eyes closed and a tender smile etched on his beautiful features.

Steve looked at the pale boy whose body was entangled with his own and smiled.

When Jason left, Steve stayed behind. He mopped up the mess with his damp running shorts and changed into a clean pair, watching the natural light drain from his office, leaving everything long and shadowy and indistinct. He sat back in his chair with his bare feet propped on the desk and crossed at the ankle. He held the business card on which Jason had scrawled his email address and cell phone number, and smiled to himself.

When the light had faded completely, Steve tugged on his

socks and shoes, clicked off the Tiffany lamp and left.

Distant heat lightning illuminated the dark, starless sky with silent flashes.

He walked slowly back to his car thinking about Jason, with his finely mounded ass, his startling directness, the hungry, open look in his eyes—and his lust for an older man. He thought about Penny, with her cold hands, her vague accusations and the hard, empty look in her eyes. He felt different somehow, like a longtime combatant who had finally negotiated a peace. And he smiled again.

When he got back to the car he found a neatly folded note on his windshield. When he unfolded it, a ring—the wide silver band with a pattern of interlocking circles—fell into his open palm. He stared at the ring and then read the note.

One man in his time plays many parts. Embrace the next age, Steve. Embrace your inner Daddy. Find strength in this ring and then pass it along to someone else who needs it. Jason.

When Steve turned into the driveway, his headlights panned across the length of Mrs. Alexander's long covered porch. Beneath the trio of old wooden fans, Penny and Mrs. Alexander sat close together on a pair of straight-backed rocking chairs, drinking iced tea from tall sweating glasses. A plate stacked high with Mrs. Alexander's signature lemon squares sat in accusatory silence on the small table between them.

Steve shut off the engine, locked the car and walked over to the edge of the yard.

"Good ev'ning, ladies," he drawled.

The two women looked at him with small, angry eyes.

He stood with his hands on his hips, loose and unwilling to be troubled by the gathering storm. He tried again. "Mrs.

Alexander, are those some of your amazing lemon squares I see there?"

They stared at him in shared silence.

"Who is she?" Penny asked.

"There is no *she*," he said.

"There have always been *shes*, Steve. Dozens of them…since long before we got married."

"Please don't start this again, Penny. There has been nobody but you for five goddamned years—"

"You've got dried cum on your shirt," Penny said. "Did that slut wipe her mouth on it after she went down on you?"

He looked down at the smeared galaxy of silvery speckles on the blue fabric of his shirt riding just above his right hip. He saw the ring on his finger, interlocking circles glinting in the porch light. He knew they had passed the point of no return. A new age was upon him.

"I want a divorce," he said without looking up.

DADDY
DRADEN

Jeff Mann

for Master JW

'm awake at first light, dim dawn in my little nest. It's chilly down here in Daddy Draden's basement den, but the blanket I snuggle in is velvety and warm. My coziness is deepened by the sound of rain—the first hard September rain drenching Roanoke, pattering on the basement's window—and by these bonds Dad has tied good and snug around my ankles and wrists. He's real handy at making comfortable cuffs out of cotton rope.

I roll onto my side, curl against the couch cushions, think of Dad and get hard. Normally, I'd just lie here till he let me loose, but this morning I aim to be bold. Last night, after two months apart, I was so excited to be with him that I came too fast. I shot as soon as he commenced to chew my nips, so the lengthy play we'd planned never came to pass; we were both disappointed. I'm hoping Dad won't mind if I take the initiative for once. Rubbing my dick, I gather my courage and then start picking at the wrist-knots with my teeth.

Pretty soon my hands are free and then my feet. I piss in the plastic bucket Dad left by the couch. Then I ready myself, hoping like hell that he won't be angry if I rouse him this early, hoping that he'll find it hot, what I got planned.

His briefs first: I don't get to see Dad very often—five or six times a year, when my partner Bob's out of town—so Dad saves his cum for me, jacking off in the same pair of briefs for weeks. These here on the floor are stained a dull brown. Their reek's rich, aged like fine wine. I ball them up and stuff them in my mouth. For a moment I close my eyes and savor the smell and taste; I picture Dad humping his hand, dumping all those yummy loads into these few inches of cloth. Then I take the roll of duct tape off the bookshelf. I plaster the tape over my lips, securing the briefs in place; I wrap the tape around my head and over my mouth again and again, five or six feet worth, good and tight, before ripping the end off. Rope next: I tie the base of my cock and balls real tight, and then the base of my balls, and then the base of my cock. My dick rears up, straining, a shaft of tight brown satin.

Prepared, I head upstairs. I'm just vain and insecure enough to slip into the hallway bathroom to check myself in the mirror. Ain't too bad, got to admit. Yep, Dad should like this. He keeps telling me I'm just his type. I stand there for a full minute, staring at myself, jacking my cock.

I'm twenty-six. My hair's a black buzz cut, widow's peak already beginning. On the sides, my beard's trimmed real close, but on my chin it thickens into a wiry black bush a good four inches long, like a Confederate soldier's or a Hell's Angel's, springing beneath the layered silver-gray tape like a dark water-fall. I'm only five foot six, stocky, pretty well muscled, with a chunky set of tits and a round little bit of belly, and I'm the hairiest guy I know. King Kong ain't got nothing on me. I used to be self-conscious about it, but I've met enough appreciative guys to be proud of my cub-pelt, the black mat that covers my chest, belly and crotch like dense moss, that caps my shoulders, dusts my back and coats my thick thighs. "Black as a country night," Dad always says. I jack myself a little more—got to admit my own looks turn me on, especially with my mouth taped shut and my cock roped up—and then I turn, checking out my chunky round butt, equally dark with fur. I reach behind me, spread my cheeks and feel cool air on my hole. I finger myself a little, hoping like hell that Dad will fuck me later.

At Dad's bedroom door, I knock softly. "Donnie?" I hear him say. "Come in." I enter, stand by his bed. My cock bobs in its web of rope; I stroke it.

Dad looks up at me, rubbing his eyes. He's so damn handsome—an older version of me, he's often said, and that's the biggest compliment he can give me. Dad's thirty-eight. He's got a burly body, a full black beard, a head of thick black hair going silvery at the temples. To my relief, he's smiling rather than frowning.

"Uhhmmm?" That's my well-taped way of saying, "Is this all right? You like this? Do I please you, Sir?"

I've been his part-time bottom for five years, so Dad understands even my grunts. "Yes, cub. Very hot." He throws back the covers, and there's his cock. We both watch as it rises to its full length and thickness. If I weren't gagged so tight, I'd lick my lips.

When Dad beckons, I fall to my knees by the bed. I lay my head on his barrel chest, snuffle the fur there, black mingled with silver, like the hair on his head. "Come on in," he says, running his fingers over my buzz cut. Now that I have permission, I climb in beside him.

It's so good to be in his bed. I love Bob and the life we've made—we've been together seven years, since undergrad days, lived together the last four, and it's all good except for the sex, which is seldom and hardly ever kinky—but even when I'm with Bob, I'm always aching for Dad to truss me up and hold me all night. I'm a restless sleeper, though, and Dad's a light sleeper, so always, after whatever rough play he gives me, he leads me to my basement nest, leaves a piss-bucket by the couch, ties me up and leaves me there till morning. Just once, I wish Dad would let me spend another night in his bed. As it is, guess I'll have to settle for this, late-night and early-morning snuggle-fests, his big arms around me, his chest hair tickling my back, his beard brushing my ears.

"Sleep all right?" Dad's fingers range between my pec-meat and cock, squeezing, stroking. I can feel his hard-on against my butt.

I nod. I'm so damn happy to be in his arms.

"I know it's raining but...want to go to that Ren Faire today? I'll bet I can find you that Viking drinking horn you've been wanting. There'll be lots of vendors."

"Uh-huh." I snuggle closer. Dad's fingers focus on my right nipple, tugging on the hair surrounding it, pinching it gently. He and I are both fantasy fans, SCA members, D&D players and comic-book nerds. Our talks are as much about the X-Men, evil sorcerers and jousting techniques as they are about daily events. The daily's kind of like vanilla sex for us: boring, at least most of the time. Give us weird instead; give us intense extremes. I think Bob doesn't mind lending me to Daddy Draden every so often just so he won't have to hear me babble about swords, mutants, Tolkien and *Dune*. Not to mention ball-gags and duct tape.

"I bet you need hurt first," Dad says. He takes my nipple

between his thumb and forefinger. His nails dig. The first wave of pain unfurls up my torso. "Ready for some hurt, Donnie-boy?"

"Uhh? Uhh?" I roll over, raising an eyebrow. In my expression is a request he's come to expect.

Dad chuckles. "Yeah, yeah, I know. It's so much better with rope, right?" I sit up, crossing my hands behind my back. He stands up, fetching cord from the floor.

"Ummmm." I sigh with relief, feeling Dad loop, tighten and knot rope around my wrists. That free will the preachers back home are always ranting about: well, when I'm Dad's captive, the burden of it disappears. Beneath the tape, around the bunched briefs, I smile, as Dad grabs another hank of rope and starts trussing my ankles. It's so great to have a Top who understands my every kinky need, who loves me for those needs instead of condemning me for a freak, like the rest of the world. All my family and friends in Giles County, the guys at the gas station where I work, if they knew a mountain boy as butch as me—hell, I'm as much a lover of pickup trucks, buttermilk biscuits and bluegrass music as any of them—if they knew I loved to be tied up, tortured and ass-raped, they'd ride me out of town on a rail. Fuck, I'd probably end up a corpse in the county dump.

Satisfied that I ain't going anywhere, Dad shoves me back onto the bed. I buck and kick, straining against my bonds, giving him the fight he relishes. "Keep still, you little redneck," Dad orders. "You're caught, boy. You're my prisoner. No way you're getting loose." He sits on my thighs, gives my chest a few punches, then sinks his teeth into my right nipple. I shout into my mouthful of rank cloth; his fingernails dig into my left pec.

Since we get together so rarely, Dad likes to take his time when he tortures me, to savor my suffering. After half an hour my eyes are wet, my shouts have turned to whimpers and sobs, my gag's sodden, and he's growling like a werewolf, low in his throat, chewing one nipple and then the other, giving my flexed pecs more sharp punches, pushing a spit-wet finger up my asshole. It's come down to agony, his teeth gnawing me raw, but I have no choice but to take it, and besides, I want to take it, I need to take it. I know Dad loves to top me because, unlike a lot of other bottoms he plays with, I can take a huge amount of abuse. I endure (albeit with a helluva lot of gagged noise) whatever he chooses to give me—flogging, tit-work, caning, cropping, whipping—for as long as he cares to continue. I've almost never begged him to stop; that's my achievement, my point of pride. "My little warrior," Dad calls me.

That's one reason, I think, that he invites me back. That, and because he knows I really care about him. The "buddy" part of "fuckbuddy" is as important for both of us as the "fuck" part. Other boys, he says, some of them just come for the rough sex. Everybody knows he's the best Top in southwest Virginia, so he has lots of bottoms clamoring to be used. But, according to Dad, half the time he's the one who feels used. According to Dad, most of them make him feel like a human dildo.

My wrists and ankles are rope-chafed by now. Exhausted, I've stopped struggling; I've surrendered completely. I lie beneath him, thrusting my ass against his probing hand, my teeth sunk in the smelly gag, moaning softly as Dad, snarling, finger-fucks me and shreds my nips.

Now he straddles my chest. He's so turned on that he pumps his dick for only a few minutes before his load spatters my face. Grinning, he rubs his cum over my tape-gag, into my beard, across my forehead. Then he rolls off me and takes my dick in his hand. I'm done in half a minute, squirting on my belly.

This might be my favorite part. Dad leaves my mouth taped,

leaves me tied hand and foot; he rolls me onto my side, cuddles up against my back, and holds me. He fondles my cum-wet beard, my cum-wet belly hair. "You're safe, boy," he whispers. "I'll take good care of you."

I want to say, "I love you, Dad. Damn, you treat me good. If it weren't for Bob and our history together, if you and me'd met first, I'd be your cub for always." But I'm still gagged, so I can't say anything, and besides, I know Dad's lonely, real lonely, and I know he wants a full-time boy bad, and I know he's been single for eight years, since he and his lost love Nate broke up and Nate moved to Texas, and I know he's afraid he's aging and may never find a permanent boy, and so, if I were to say what I want to say, it'd just be harder on both of us when I go home to Bob later this afternoon. Instead, I snuggle back against him and rub my taped mouth against his hand.

I guess closeness feels dangerous to both of us sometimes. Suddenly Dad sits up, breaking the charged silence. "I make you do bad things, don't I, boy?" he says, loosening my wrist-knots. "That liquid-courage bottle of red wine you always bring along. The Chinese buffet last night, with all those fattening crab rangoons and egg rolls and General Tso's chicken. And then BDSM. And now, guess what? Yes! How'd my boy like to hit Krispy Kreme for breakfast?"

I nod happily, giving an enthusiastic "Uhhhh-*huh*!" as Dad removes the ropes about my wrists and starts freeing my feet. Sometimes I wish I could be his slave, his boy, all the time. Other times I think the once-every-couple-months thing is best. I'm afraid if I were here all the time, I'd bore him. As it is, we spend our lives hungry for each other, and I guess that ain't a bad way to live.

* * *

When I'm alone, and sometimes even when Bob and I are doing it—which ain't too often these days—I think of Daddy Draden. I run through them, scene after scene over the last five years. Memories as hot as them never fail to get me off fast. Listen, man. I'll tell you a few.

It's snowing the night Draden and I meet face-to-face. I'm living alone, in that broken-down house on Airport Road; Bob's still living in West Virginia, and we're meeting on weekends. Bob knows how much I need kink and how much I need to bottom sometimes, so he tolerates it when I cruise leather and bear websites. I guess he figures if I can find someone trust-worthy, he won't have to bother with tying me up or topping me anymore. He just ain't into it, since he's pretty much a bottom himself, and I guess that's all right—or it'll have to be—since he treats me so good otherwise.

Anyway, Daddy Draden and I meet online, start chatting—he lives only an hour away—and one night our planning comes together, and I'm watching the clock, a little drunk on Jack, and the snow's coming down, hard enough that I'm afraid he'll cancel, but there's the knock at the door I've been waiting for. And that's how I see my Dad for the first time. I open the door and shiver; I've followed his orders and am wearing nothing but boxer shorts because they turn him on. He's standing on the stoop in the snowfall. He's dressed in black work boots, black jeans, black T-shirt, black leather biker jacket and biker's cap. He looks down at me and grins—he's a good foot taller than me. "Damn, boy, you're even hairier than I thought!"

I look up into his dark eyes and grin back. "Good to meet you, Sir. I hope you like my fur."

Draden nods; we shake hands. I invite him in, offer him Jack. He wants beer instead. I keep drinking bourbon, because

I'm scared and excited and I always like a little buzz going when I submit to a Top, especially a new one I don't know real well yet. Don't take long before he's wrapped a short chain around my neck and padlocked it, so I guess I'm his for the evening. Then he's behind me, holding me close, one big hand clamped over my mouth, the other tugging my tits. I've already told him online that my nips are my ON buttons, and he wastes no time taking advantage of that fact. I love the pressure of his hand over my mouth; I love the pain building up in my chest; I love this feeling of being mastered by an older, larger man.

We're on my bed now, frost feathering like maidenhair ferns across the bedroom window, the spruce trees outside covered with white. We're both naked. I don't know it now, but this is a scene I'm going to be jacking off to for the next half a decade. Draden has me on my elbows and knees. My hands are tied together and anchored to the headboard with a short rope-tether. I've got my hairy butt in the air; Dad's strapped a ball-gag in my mouth and I'm drooling like a motherfucker, head down in the sheets while Dad kneels behind me, puts on a rubber and lubes us up. It hurts bad at first—I ain't that used to being fucked, and Dad's got an eight-incher and thick to boot—but soon enough we're rocking together, back and forth, he's thrusting in and out, I'm grunting like the happy pig I am.

Dad cums up my butt; I cum in his hand about the same time. We snuggle, and oh, god, is that sweet, to be held so tender by a man who'd used me rough like a whore only minutes before.

"The noises you make when you get fucked sound interrogative, boy." Dad chuckles. "'Uhhh? Ummmm?' Sounds like you're asking me a question."

"I'm saying, 'Please, Daddy, would you plow me harder and faster?'" I say, head on his shoulder.

Dad laughs, wraps his arms around me, holds me tight.

He spends the night, since the snow has got so bad. But, dammit, I toss and turn too much, snore too loud. That's the last night we sleep together, though it's the first, thank god, of many tasty-as-hell nights we play.

The movie's *Ladyhawke*. It's one of Dad's favorites, but I haven't seen it before. Tonight I'm watching it with him, but in kind of an unusual way.

He's lounging on the couch in shorts and a T-shirt. I'm naked, tied to a chair beside the couch. He leaves me tied like this sometimes when I'm around in the summer and he needs to cut the grass. Tonight I spend several hours in this position. My wrists are bound behind the chair, as are my elbows. He's got loads of rope wrapped around my chest and upper arms and belly, securing me to the chair back so tight I can't hardly move. My legs are spread, my thighs roped to the chair-seat and my ankles roped to the back legs. He's got a butt plug up my ass, and he's got tweezer clamps hanging from my nips. Occasionally, in between scenes—guy changing to wolf, girl changing to hawk, gotta admit it's a pretty cool movie, so no wonder Dad likes it—he pauses the DVD, pulls the plug-gag out of my mouth and tips a beer to my lips. When I'm done gulping and thanking him, he gags me again and starts tugging and twisting the clamps till my numbed tits burn and my eyes water. Then he sprawls back on the couch and starts up the DVD. It's the hottest goddamn way to watch a movie, man. Take my word for it.

"Get that butt up in the air."

I'm belly down, tied spread-eagle to Dad's bed. He pushes the button on the remote control. The electric cock ring zaps my crotch. I yelp. Obedient, I angle my ass higher.

"Beg for it, Donnie-boy. Ask for more."

Dad's got a camo bandana tied real tight between my teeth, so I can't talk clear, but he doesn't care. "Please, Sir," I mumble around the cloth my pained shouts have soaked with spit. "Please give me more, Sir. Cane my butt more, please, Sir."

Again the zap of the cock ring. I let loose another yelp, like a kicked lap dog. Then the cane comes down on my bare ass, again and again, first one cheek, then the other, then both together. *Pow pow pow pow pow pow pow.* The pain builds, sharp and steady, thin and hot. Feels like I'm being sliced open by a flaming pocketknife, a narrow blade cleaving me the way an axe does oak.

Am I bleeding yet? Sure feels like it. I want to beg Dad to stop, but I'm too proud to do that. Instead, I squint my eyes shut and bite down on my gag so hard my jaw commences to ache. I'd like to cry for him, just break loose and sob, let long-held-back tears roll down my face—we both want that bad—but seems like I can't, no matter how much I suffer. Men where I come from, we were brought up never to cry. I want broken bad, and Dad wants bad to break me, but so far—five years of on-and-off torture—it ain't happened. Most I can manage is some wet-rimmed eyes and a few choked-back sobs. Some part of me just can't let go.

The sharp blows pause. "More, boy?" Dad's voice is deep and kind.

Zap!

"Yes," I squeak against my gag.

"Louder."

Zap!

"*Yes!*" I yell. "Yes, *please*! More, Sir. *More!*"

The cane descends again, with a swishing sound that makes me wince even before it connects with my buttcheeks. Pressing my face into the sheets, I lift my rear end higher still. I want to be beat so bad it hurts to sit. Dad knows that, and he's determined to oblige.

First time Daddy Draden mummified me, he let me sleep on the floor at the foot of his bed. But again I disturbed his rest. Bleary-eyed the next morning, he growled, "You flopped around like a damn fish all night." So tonight I spend in the guest room, on a big tarp so I won't wet the floor if I have to piss in the middle of the night. He's wrapped me real tight in yards and yards of clear plastic wrap, so I'm encased from my ankles to my neck, with my hands imprisoned at my sides. I'm already sweating a ton as he reinforces the wrap with duct tape, circling my body at the ankles, knees, waist, above and below my pecs. He stands astraddle me now, bit-gag in hand, looking down, a gaze both stern and fond.

"You can take this till morning?"

Beneath the plastic, sweat's beading in my belly hair and chest hair.

"Yes, Sir."

Dad pushes the rubber bit between my teeth and buckles the straps tight behind my head. "This gag will let you yell for help if you panic or get into trouble. Okay? I'll be right down the hall if you need me."

I nod. He's mummified me many times before. I'll be fine. By morning, I'll have pissed myself at least twice, after all the beer I drank tonight. He'll jack me off, cut me loose, and help me to the shower, and I'll feel clean and new, like a butterfly crawling from a chrysalis or Christ stumbling from the tomb, shucking off darkness and the grave.

Dad falls to his knees beside me. He kisses my forehead. Then he pulls out a pocketknife. If he were anyone else, I'd be fucking scared—lying here immobilized while a big guy pulls a knife—but no, I just lie real still as he cuts, slow and careful. Pretty soon my cock and balls are exposed, cool air drying the sweat, and my nips too. The plastic wrap's so tight my nips bulge out like little balloons, stand up like pink cones. Since almost all my skin's covered by this insulating cocoon, seems like the sensation normally spread over my body is concentrated in the pinpoints of my tits. Dad knows this. He makes love to them, gentle, not rough, with his fingers and tongue, till I'm about to go fucking crazy with the sweet feel of it. He jacks me too, slow and tight, and now I'm moaning, thrusting into his fist, pushing my chest against his mouth.

I'm about four strokes short of cumming when the warm, wet feel of his lips on my nips disappears. "Sweet dreams." Dad gives my dick a farewell squeeze and stands. He clicks off the lights and leaves me here on the floor, cock bobbing, sweat trickling down my sides.

Here I am strapped hand and foot between two columns in Dad's basement, nakedness stretched out in a taut X, whimpering as he adds another clothespin to the slew already fixed in lines across my chest and belly. My cock and balls are covered, bristling with pins like a chestnut burr.

"That's forty-nine," he says, adding one above my navel. "And here's fifty." He lifts the final pin to my face.

I know what's coming, and it's gonna hurt like holy hell. I crease my brow in a silent plea for mercy. I shake my head, and a big gob of slobber spills through the O-ring gag, over my chin and onto the floor. Dad squeezes the pin open, then slowly closes it on the thin wall of flesh separating my nostrils. I guess the jagged little noises I'm making now would be called sniveling, but I don't care how pathetic I sound, it hurts so much.

Dad leaves me like that, coated with what feels like burning embers, while he checks his email and starts dinner.

Okay, that's enough. Hell, you get it, right? They go on and on, the past scenes we've shared. If Daddy Draden were to tell me to get lost tomorrow, I'd still have memories enough to keep me horned up for years. But tonight reminds me that what we have ain't just hot. It's real. Me suffering for him helps us both get through other kinds of pain.

"He stood me up again," Dad says. It's a chilly January evening, and we're about to dive into the carry-out we just fetched home. It's a running joke, that Sonic's "our place." I figure, if I'm gonna have me some edgy sex, I might as well live it up, throw the diet out the window and indulge a little, so, two times out of three, we hit Sonic for burgers, foot-long hot dogs, and tater tots before the beating begins. "The little bastard never showed."

"Which one?"

"The ex-marine who wanted me to kidnap him. I sat in that motel parking lot for two hours, but he never showed."

Tonight, as we sit around the kitchen table, munching our greasy haul, Dad talks and I listen. He's lonelier, more depressed than ever. He has good reasons to be grim. On top of a shit load of crap at work—most of his coworkers at the DMV sound like morons—his attempts to find a regular boy are going nowhere. He's been chatting with single guys, guys who might be there for him all the time, as I can't. They're fucking flakes, every one. I'd like to break their heads. They flirt, they promise things, they get his hopes up, and then they don't show up, or, if they do, they're spoiled, ungrateful, selfish. One of them, after the lightest of floggings, ran out of the house hysterical, the crazy queen. One stole some money. One gave him crabs. As much as

I love to suck Dad off, or take a load of his cum up my butt after a good beating, well, it's harder and harder for him to get it up. Depression erodes his sex drive, he says, and antidepressants do the same. If he can manage to jack off after he tortures me, we're both lucky. He hasn't fucked me in over a year.

One of these nights, he's gonna be so sad he won't want me anymore. But not tonight, thank god. When Dad finishes his last tater tot and I finish my dog and my glass of wine, he leads me into the playroom. I'm naked now, on my back on the padded bondage table, ankles tied to the legs, hands tied together beneath it. Dad's tasty-rank briefs are crammed in my mouth again; layers of duct tape are plastered over my lips and wrapped around the bench, real snug so I can't move my head. Dad's in full leather, beating my chest and belly flush-red with a riding crop. We're both relishing my muffled screams. We're both still yet blessed. When his arm gets tired and he lets me loose, I fall to my knees and kiss his boots.

"Lick," Dad says, so I do, lapping the shiny leather shinier.

"This helps, cub," Dad says. "I'm glad you're here."

Ten months later, it's my turn to talk. Dad listens, snuggling with me on the couch. I've just been laid off, the economy's so bad I can't find another job, and my savings won't last long. My little cat's sick; she's got cancer and it's too far gone to operate. Bob's been real cranky, we've been fighting a lot, and we don't hardly ever have sex anymore. I'm just glad I have a brawny Dad like Draden to hold me tonight.

"I'm done," I say, tipping the fifth of Jack to my lips. "Sorry you had to hear all that. You know we hillbillies can't tell a tale of woe any way other than real long."

Dad stands, then pulls me to my feet. He takes the bottle from me, puts it on the table. He crooks a finger under the slave collar I always wear at his place. "I told you I'd take care of you, Donnie," he says. "Come on." He leads me down the hall to the playroom.

Soon I'm stripped and face up against the St. Andrews cross. Dad locks my wrists and ankles in leather cuffs, so I'm standing spread-eagle. He ball-gags and blindfolds me. He starts slow with a light paddling, the wood warming up my asscheeks. The flogger's next, heavy strands of leather caressing my shoulders and back. Gradually the blows get more severe. Now it feels like someone's punching me. I gasp and drool, arch my back and beg for more.

"Single-tail now," Dad says. The whip's hissing through the air, sharp stinging across my shoulder blades, fire-welts cutting into my back. I pant and shake.

Dad moves the action to my ass. The paddle's no longer a warming glow. The stiff wooden whacks come harder and faster. I bite down on the ball and choke back my cries. I want him to stop now; god, how it hurts, worse than ever before, but I'm his boy and he calls me his little warrior and I want to take it all, want to be brave for him, and now, god, the single-tail again, slicing my shoulders, "You're bleeding, boy. Want me to stop?" I shake my head, shout out *"No!"* and oh, fuck, at last, beneath my blindfold I can feel tears trickling, and fuck, oh, fuck, I'm so angry, scared and sad; how it hurts, bound here, bound down in this body; at last something snaps inside me, and the tears are gushing, and I'm sobbing and slobbering, spit's running down my chin, and I'm shaking and jerking, the chains that hold me down are rattling, and I'm crying and I can't stop.

The blows cease. There's the sound of the whip hitting the floor, of clothes being peeled off. Dad strokes the throbbing burn of my back, and his fingers' soft touch makes me jolt and tremble and cry harder. Dad stands behind me, holding me inside his nakedness. He tousles my hair, pulls off the blindfold. Light floods my eyes. Snot's running from my nose, and Dad suddenly has a Kleenex in his hand. "No, please, it's nasty," I mumble, but Dad holds the tissue to my nose anyway, and I blow and snort. I'm laughing and crying at the same damn time now, as Dad unbinds my hands and feet, then loosens my gag-straps and pulls the dripping ball from my mouth.

I turn from the cross and my knees buckle and I fall into his arms and cry even harder. We lie on the floor, hugging one another tight, my face buried in his chest hair. I cry some more. Finally I stop. Dad helps me up. He leads me to his bed. He rubs lotion into my back and ass. "Yes, cub," he says, spooning me. "Tonight you can stay here with me."

I sleep sound, waking only once to find Dad's arms still around me. First light, I get up to piss. I stare at the bathroom mirror. My eyes are bloodshot and my sinuses aching, thanks to all those tears. I turn, studying my reflection. Black bruises and red welts cover my shoulders, back and butt, like someone had spilled pokeberry ink or scrawled red sentences into my skin.

Today, I ain't in any hurry to get back to the sadness at home. Think I'll take the long way back, up over the mountains of Craig County. I'll stop at my favorite down-home diner in New Castle and get me some coffee and some biscuits and sausage gravy, and I'll sit there, listening to bow-hunters in camo talk about the bucks they brought down, and all they'll see is a stocky little redneck with a bushy black beard, dressed in jeans and cowboy boots and a Virginia Tech Hokies baseball cap and a Led Zeppelin T-shirt, and I'll be what I seem to be and very much not what I seem to be, with these wounds Dad left hidden beneath my clothes, each mark a reminder of all the gifts he's given me.

"Get in here, Donnie-boy," I hear Daddy Draden growl from the bedroom.

Don't take Dad long to tie my hands behind my back and fuck my face till he cums. The load he dumps in my mouth tastes like hope. Milk of human kindness: now I get the phrase. Dad drowses a little and then pulls out, slaps my cheeks with his dick, lets me lick the post-cum ooze from his slit.

I'm on the road now. We've said our good-byes. God knows when we'll meet again or what'll happen next. Maybe Bob will get tired of me coming home all beat up, ask me to move out. I suspect he's already sick of how little sex we have, and I am too. Maybe Dad will find a full-time boy, fall in love, move away. Maybe Dad and I will end up together.

Who the hell knows? If being tied up and tortured has taught me anything, it's to live in my body as much as I can, focus on the present, not dwell on what I can't change or control. Today the maple leaves are orange and red, the coves are white with mist, and the wet fields streaming by either side the road are steaming in the sun. I roll down the truck-window to feel autumn air on my face. I turn on the radio—that hot Zac Brown's singing "Free." Today, that's how I feel, thanks to Dad, thanks to the bruises on my back and butt. I'm young and clean and light and free. I'm that dew-glitter on the pasture grass, on the verge of evaporating, ready to rise into the sun.

FATHER AND SON TAG TEAM
(THAT SUMMER! THAT CAMP! THAT COUSIN!)

Jack Fritscher

I woke up in this story suckling his big dick. When you're eighteen and still in your wonder years, like I was that summer of 2001, you do strange things in your sleep, like kick off all the sheets and dream buck naked with your prick up hard as the flashlight you hide to read porn at night under the blankets.

Older counselors like Taggart, who was nineteen-plus (as in *plus ten inches*), love to pull tricks on younger guys. You know, when you're out playing counselor at some Camp Gitchygoomee and it's the last week of the season, after all the campers have packed up their sweaty jockstraps and nylon Speedos and headed back home. I missed some of them: the best of the cool young dudes all tanned and buffed and trained for their football, wrestling and swimming teams back home. The camp was deserted. Quiet. More beautiful than ever. We had maybe a week's more work to do. Almost alone. Me and Tag.

I kept sucking, my eyes tightly closed, pretending I was asleep. I felt Tag's big blond thighs straddling my chest. Maybe I was dreaming. All summer long, I'd lusted after him. He was a diver, six-two,185, lean-muscled and handsome. A dreamboat. When he practiced his approaches on the diving board, his long defined toes striding the length to the tip where he bounced up and down on the edge, my eyes never left his crotch, the tight wet, big bulge of his red trunks, the famous nylon Speedos I once stole and sniffed and shoved into my mouth to suck out the taste of his big cock.

Tag hung ten easy. Eyes closed I knew that. I felt his soft dick hardening in my mouth. I worked my lips around the velvet head, almost afraid to open my eyes, for fear I'd wake up and he'd be no more than an early morning piss-hard dream vanishing in the late-summer dawn. But his dick gelling from soft to hard in my mouth, the taste and smell of him—hey, I knew the real thing.

So I opened my eyes, and, shit! It wasn't Taggart at all!

Well, it was, but it wasn't the Taggart I thought. It was, I swear to god, the other Taggart! It was his dad, who had been a big stud at sixteen, had fathered Young Tag at seventeen and was still married to his wife, Verna Taggart. They all ran Camp Gitchygoomee with Verna knowing everything, especially book-work and her place.

The night before, we had celebrated Big Tag's thirty-sixth birthday, telling him the truth that he didn't look a day over twenty-six. You get the picture. He was the coach, the daddy, the husband, the stud. The Taggarts, father and son, were a special breed of the biggest cocks I ever saw. So I looked real surprised, and twice as pleased, when I opened my eyes and found Big Tag threading my throat. I'd worshipped Big Tag from afar all summer: *him* swimming naked in the pool, endless laps of backstroke with his long cock cutting the water, sluicing its own wake; *him*, in Fort Cobb, which is what we called the main toilet, flipping his big dick over the gray sheet-metal piss trough; *him* groping himself in his nylon shorts around the evening campfire. I saw where Young Tag, who no one ever dared call Little Tag, got his size and I knew why Verna hung around her men smiling no matter what went on.

Between his thighs, Big Tag sported a real handsome piece of blue-veined meat. I'm talking twelve inches of blond cock, maybe nine inches circumference, which I think is about the exact circumference of my mouth stretched open to its widest cocksucking ring, just wide enough, I could tell, for the mushroom head, when he pulled it out of my mouth and with both fists waved it back and forth across my face, flushed that juicy hot purple peculiar to blond cocks.

He smiled and said, "This is your wake-up call, Sonny."

I remember everything exactly.

"Are you surprised?"

I grinned like the cocksucker I've always been and shook my head *no* and stretched my tongue for his lubing piss slit.

"Are you disappointed?"

I snorted one of those you-gotta-be-kidding laughs and he drove the head of his cock right straight through my smile and laid pipe down my throat.

When a good-looking summer-camp director who stands six-four and weighs in at a solid 225 spreads his jock-thighs across my chest while the morning sun spotlights the blond hair on his pecs and forearms, I know, like the joke about where the two-thousand-pound canary can sit, that any man that much larger than life can, if he wants, sit on my face and pedal my ears till the cows come home. I worship big dick and Big Tag loved adoration. His cock played my vocal chords like the devil plays fiddle.

"You want it, huh? You little cocksucker."

Beat me, daddy. Eight to the bar. Obviously, father and son, probably playing "tag" together, had pillow-talked about me behind my back, and that's always the best kind of talk. Besides, I'd read some of the graffiti written on the walls of Fort Cobb.

Big Tag spread my jaws and drill-pumped me inch by inch, working deeper, bringing tears to my eyes and choking sounds to my throat.

"Your throat's too tight too soon," he said.

He worked me loose so he could go deeper. Six inches was easy to handle. I slurped him like a pro. Inches seven and eight came harder, but not that hard.

Early that summer his son had broken the deep-cherry back in my throat where a hard cock exits down and out the back of your mouth and passes through the first gate leading to your guts.

I worried about inches nine through twelve. Like, could I swallow that much cock? I'd never quite got fully impaled on his son's ten-incher; but then Young Tag was rougher getting his nut. Big Tag was smoother, more experienced. He talked dirty to me—I'm a sucker for verbal sex—almost hypnotizing me, fuck-talking, building my passion for the triumph of swallowing his total manhood down to the root. He was so intense a talker he convinced me to go for it, to dare to take it. He slipped me inch nine, then pulled out, real slow and gentle, and immediately drove back in, knocking off inch ten, surprising me, smiling a small sneer that curled up under his bushy blond moustache. The sweet blond hairs of his crotch were still two inches from my face, and I knew he wouldn't shoot till my nose was buried in his groin, and he was in me a foot deep, his full twelve inches.

My own cock was bouncing fast in my hand. Big Tag, who always kept a neat pinch of Copenhagen under his lower lip, turned and spit slow sweet tobacco drool down on my dick.

"Beat your meat," he said. "You'll find room for my last two inches in your own cock. When your own cock gets cock-crazy, you'll let me in."

He wasn't forcing anything. I mean this wasn't a rape fantasy. It was real. It was the greatest thing two men can do. It was six-thirty in the morning. He had his horsecock planted ten inches down my throat, and he was coaching me, like the summer coach he was, to take more of what he had to offer.

My daddy never raised me to be nobody's fool.

I know now what I learned that morning. There is one sin in life: when a man offers you a hard twelve-inch cock and you do not take it all. I didn't need much coaching. I was such a cock pig, I wished that Young Tag was there, son and father, twenty-two inches of cock between them. But it wasn't that fantasy either. It was reality. Sweaty sheets. Dripping armpits. Nasty talk. Bouncing bull balls. Hairy chest. Dropdead looks, blond hair, three-days' unshaved bristle. His big cock pumping my face, slowly, his lean hips and waist rocking over me, my hand working my cock, knowing I could cum for the first time in my life with twelve inches of big blond cock pistoning my tonsils, if only I could split two more inches of ch-ch-cherry throat.

Life, my daddy told me, is mind over matter. Thanks, Dad. My cock beat on the cusp of cumming. I looked up at Big Tag. The brilliant morning sun hit him, lit him, over me like a golden stud. I realized the most private part of that man was deep in me, and I wanted him deeper. I groaned guttural sounds and looked up at him and wrinkled my forehead and nodded. That was all he needed. I beat my dick. He drove half-inch by half-inch into my mouth.

At eleven inches he paused, then began not to penetrate, but to fuck my face. From slow to hard, he toppled from friendly persuasion to bucking passion. He fell over my face like a jock doing push-ups and pinioned my arms on the pillow above my head. I thought I'd choke or die, but I didn't. I did what he wanted. What I wanted. I opened and swallowed. He face-fucked me past eleven inches to the full twelve.

I felt his blond crotch slam solid against my lips. He was home. He fully holstered his rod in my throat. He worked me wild. I felt his cock throb and expand in the sheath of my throat and feared I'd drown if he shot his load into my lungs, but I didn't care, 'cuz he'd give me mouth-to-mouth and hold me in his arms, and at the precise moment when he blew, my own cock, untouched, shot across my belly, sort of like his huge cock was inside my cock, and his white cum came boiling up out of my nose, my mouth, and, yeah, out of my cock. His cum shooting out of my cock. His cum that turned into Young Tags with ten-inch dicks. His twelve-inch cock, seeming inside my dick, stretched my own rod out a full foot so my dick skin strained like a rubber stuffed to bursting with a studbull cock. I could feel what it felt like to pack a twelve-inch rod!

Oh, god. You get the picture. I did. I do.

That summer I had more "Tags" on me than a Blue Light Special at the WalMart. Young Tag had a cousin, Big Tag's brother's son, Lawayne MacRory Taggart, who everybody called "MacTag," because he said so. He was tough and streetwise and he liked to wrestle, freestyle, slam-banging and clowning like the pro wrestlers on TV. He'd gone beyond his once-beloved Hulk Hogan and was idolizing the muscular Sonny Butts, the buffed and black Jamal "Reggie Reggae" Deshaw, and the outrageous tag team, the Slap Warriors.

He fed the campers a liar-liar-pants-on-fire line about how he wrestled on TV, billing himself the "Masked Counselor." The campers loved it. Especially when he pulled a black wrestling mask over his blond head and climbed into the ring with one of the tougher, huskier, older ones, both of them stripped down to nylon briefs and wrestling boots, bouncing off the ropes, MacTag picking the kid up, throwing him across his shoulders and spinning him around, slamming him to the padded canvas, flopping across the kid, full body, pinning his shoulders, while the crowd went wild screaming, "Next! Next! Me next!"

MacTag was their chance to act out a fantasy. Now I know.

One night that last week after camp, I stood in my Speedos in the door of MacTag's cabin. I could feel the full moon falling warm on my shoulders and back. MacTag looked up from the table where by the light of a Coleman lantern he was reading *Leaves of Grass*, buck naked, playing with himself.

"Next!" I whispered.

He smiled, closed the book and stood up. He was a Taggart all right. He had the dick. He slow-walked toward me in that hip-ball-and-joint walk that athletes with powerful thighs and bubblebutts take as their trademark stroll. His dick swung easy between his legs, halfway to his knees, soft yet, but with the swelling blue veins that are surefire prediction of the cockquake to come. He walked straight up to me. He stood so close I smelled the sweet summer sweat glistening on his chest, running down his armpits, beading on the hair of his muscular arms. "You sure you wanna be next?" His smile had that kind of killer sneer that Brad Pitt smiled in *Thelma and Louise*.

"Anything you can dish out, I can eat."

He snorted a laugh, but I could tell he appreciated my bluff of trying to talk tough like wrestlers do between matches on TV when they scream at the camera about what slime their next opponents are and how they're going to kill them with a metal folding chair.

"Can you eat this, Sonny?" MacTag wrapped both hands

around his rising cock. "You want it here in the cabin," he said, "or do you want to go out to the ring and get beat up a little? You know, just a little punishment. Nothing serious that a ten-inch hot-beef injection can't cure. Just maybe a little fantasy in the squared circle to make things hotter. A knee to the groin. A half nelson..."

"A full nelson." What was I saying? *Half nelson. Full nelson. Ricky Nelson.* I wanted him. I wanted every inch he had. I wanted his fantasy inside my fantasy.

"Yeah. Good. A full nelson too. Maybe even a little choking. I mean I can tell by the look in your eye you want me to be the Bad Guy. You think I can be the Bad Guy?"

MacTag raised up his arms and flexed. His biceps popped like Teenage Mr. America. Blue veins ran down to the blond forest in his juicy armpits. He crunched out a Most Muscular pose, like a wrestling warrior taking center mat. His chest and shoulders pumped big, his abs rippled, and his dick, excited by the full flush of his body, cantilevered another inch up toward total erection: straight up his belly past his navel.

"You are definitely bad." My cock tented my Speedos. Faced with his ten inches, maybe more, I reached for my cock knowing my secret I never told anybody, that every inch of big cock I sucked made my cock grow that much bigger, slowly but surely. At sixteen, I measured six inches all by my bonesome lonesome. At eighteen, I was eight-plus. These encounters were working. Some cocks make you larger. By the time I was thirty, I projected I'd be hung at least...

"You fuckin' little Size Freak." MacTag said it in the appreciative way a big-hung guy says a line like that when he knows he's on to a cocksucker who won't waste his time sucking down anything less than eight inches. Believe it or not, some cocksuckers won't do big dicks. Or can't. Or worse, tongue-and-lip

only the tips like most of those lipstick dollies do in straight
suck films.

Go figure.

MacTag, faster than I could think, picked me up, throwing
my legs over his shoulders, just like that statue of ancient wrestlers, hanging my head upside down facing his big juicy dick.
"Suck it, fuck-face!" he said. He knew from the walls of Fort
Cobb I liked to hear bullies talk nasty. "Suck it! Or I'll body-
slam you to the fucking floor."

Upside down, I took the flared head of his cock into my
mouth, figuring its circumference more than seven inches. He
bounced me on his shoulder with one hand, banging the back
of my head with the other, kind of dribbling my noggin like a
basketball down on his rod. He was teaching me a whole new
sixty-nine. Then he flipped me up over his shoulders and swung
me in full-circle airplane spins.

God! He was strong. His dick stuck out, proud of his performance. Sex-wrestling turned him on. Suddenly he raised me,
pressed me, by the sheer strength of his upper body to arms'
length, high in the air, above his head.

I whipped my dick. This was new! This was sexplay! This
was what the big boys do!

Then like the surprise thrill on an E-Ticket ride in an X-rated
park, he slam-dropped me like a feather to the floor. As crazy
as it was, everything seemed in slow motion. He threw his big
thighs across my chest, took one of my wrists in each hand,
stretched my arms out and slid his drooling cock across my pecs
and toward my face, where he buried it headfirst in my mouth
before starting the snake's slow slithering down my throat.

Everything felt awful comfortable. I realized I wasn't on
the hardwood floor. I was pinioned on a mattress on the floor.
MacTag was a class act, but how did he do that?

I heard a loud slap. The kind of slap one strong flat palm makes striking another when two men slap five.

"Tag team!" MacTag said.

"Tag team!" Young Tag said.

I tried to say, "Oh, shit," around MacTag's pumping cock.

Young Tag had been napping in one of the upper bunks while MacTag read. He'd tossed the four single mattresses to the floor.

"Tie this on," he said to MacTag. He handed him a camou-flage-green bandana folded to a headband. "We're the Blond Mercenaries," Young Tag said. "We got plenty between us because we got twenty inches between us! Whoa!"

"He wants a full nelson," MacTag said.

Young Tag obliged. From behind me, his strong arms slipped under my armpits and he clasped his hands behind my neck, positioning my mouth perfectly for a straight-on fuck from MacTag, who never took his dick out of my mouth. Young Tag's dick was rock hard between my shoulder blades.

Was I in heaven or wha-u-u-t?

MacTag was shorter and stockier than Young Tag who himself, being a swimmer, was leaner and not quite as tall as Big Tag, who, I mentioned, was six-four and 225. They were like three studs in the same gene bank and all of them hung like sonsabitches with thirty-two inches among the three of them.

The Tag Team worked my legs, squeezed me in bear hugs, double-teamed me, both of them working their own hard cocks, standing over me, talking dirty to me about their big animal cocks, dropping down with one knee across my chest, showing me the dick I wanted, teasing me with their huge pricks, then raising me up with aerial tactics, hammering me into the canvas like pro maniacs, always pulling their punches, squeezing tight on the choke holds, taking turns beating my face for real

with their ten-inch cocks. I crumpled under the "brutal" bull-
dogging; but I wanted more.

This was a championship bout of inches.

We must have brawled off and on for almost an hour, which
is a really long time when you're wrestling or being mauled by
two strong young cousins acting out on you the pro-wrestling
fantasy they've played so often together.

Finally, they pinned me. Again. Their weight on me felt like
an avalanche of hot young jocks. Their dicks ran stout, stayed
hard, pulsed for release. They slap-tagged each other's hands
and knelt up over my face, taking turns fucking my mouth, the
taste of each distinctive, yet with that undertaste of the sweet,
sweet, sweet Taggart genes.

As much as they liked my mouth, they liked the mirror they
were to each other: the heavier-muscled blond wrestler and the
lean-muscled blond swimmer, so much alike in their sunny
good-looking faces. Kneeling over my face, my mouth tonguing
their furry balls, they sucked tongues and fingered nipples and
beat their meat, building their passion to a climax.

Down between their thighs, I watched their studplay: kissing
mouths and licking tits and rubbing biceps; both pairs of blond
balls beginning to swell, rolling and rising, left nut over right,
then back again, with the dorsal veins on the underside of their
almost-twin cocks growing thick with potency, both cousins
totally into each other, talking dirty in short one-word grunts,
saying, "dick," "big dick," "big blond dick," "beat it," "big
fucking arms," "sweat," "dick," "juicy hard dick," "lick,"
"suck," "gonna take you on the mat, motherfucker," "gonna
cum," "on his face," "shoot it on his fucking face." And they
did, both cousins, locked in their embrace of arms and chests
and faces, beating their meat over my face, squirting the loads
of their young, blond ten-inch dicks into my mouth held open

wider than a choirboy stuck on the fourth note of "O Holy Night."

I came without touching myself. I was eighteen too, remember, and this was summer's end, and nothing, I was certain, would ever be this much fun again. Not even when we became grown-ups.

We fell together into a pig pile of sweat and cum and cock. MacTag and Young Tag dozed with me sandwiched between them. The only sound was the buzz of the Coleman lantern and the crazed moth that circled it.

I heard footsteps come the final three steps up the cabin stairs. The cousins' two pairs of sleeping blond arms wrapped around my head kept me in traction. The footsteps, heavy even in Reeboks, stepped directly behind my head. I looked up over my eyebrows, and I gulped.

It was Big Tag grinding his twelve-inch keeper in his hand. I could tell he was on the last ten strokes of cumming. He had been watching us all along. He raised his fingers to his lips to keep my silence. His fine big body arched back, displaying his massive cock, one hand working his nipples left and right. Then he stood almost at military brace, and with a silent tremor, holding in his cumshout, wanting to shoot the surprise of his load on the pair of unsuspecting, dozing blonds, gritting his breath, blowing air between his teeth, he shot the load of the father on his son, his nephew and me, thick blasts of cum splashing down on us three boys like hot rain in August.

I don't need to send you a fish-camp postcard. You get the picture. I have the pictures. Like, I still have them. In my head. In my dick. In my scrapbook. One picture in particular: the four of us, Tag and Big Tag and MacTag and me, standing nearly naked, our big dicks half hanging out of our Speedos, all in a line, with our arms around each other's shoulders like we would always be best friends forever together.

Verna, I remember, snapped the picture. "Now you'll have a snapshot," she said proudly to me, "to remember how it was this summer with you and my three big guys."

THE LESSON

Kyle Lukoff

Look, I swear I'm not some sort of crazy hippie. I believe in the laws of physics, and the theory of evolution and in washing my hair. But I really, really love talking about astrology. Like, my last lover? He was a Libra. I am never doing that again. Scorpios I'll hook up with, but that's about it. And don't even talk to me about an Aries.

I never used to believe in this stuff, but one day a customer came up to me while I was at work and said, "So. You're a Gemini, aren't you."

I gaped at her. "No! I mean, maybe. Yes. How did you know?"

"I could just tell," she said. "The way you're standing, the way you hold yourself. How quickly you talk. How young you look. I analyze people's charts for a living, you know, and you just give off this...glow that only Geminis have."

I smiled, absurdly proud of myself for being born in June. I'm still less than half-convinced that this stuff is true, but Geminis are the Twins, right? Multifaceted, two-faced, double trouble in every way. So it should be no surprise that I have two lovers, and that they are as different from each other as shadow and sunlight.

I met my Daddy Howard first. He's forty-five, older than me by about fifteen years. He's a Taurus, and even looks like a bull; medium height, compact build, salt-and-pepper hair, wise brown eyes and a rare but warm smile. He's a leatherman of the old school, with his keys and black hankie always in his left pocket. I was intimidated by him at first but quickly discovered the humble, generous, kind-hearted spirit beneath his gruff exterior.

We love each other very much. Sometimes he takes me to hard places, scary places, where my demons come out to trip me up and pull me down. He's flogged me until I've cried and caned me until I bruised, confined me in a rubber sleepsack and hand-cuffed me to his belt. But he always takes me back afterward, kisses me and tells me that I'm his good boy, makes me proud to wear his marks. Enveloped in his arms or curled up against his chest, I feel safe and warm and content.

I was interested in leather and sadomasochism before I met him, and I had even played around with it a bit, but he took my passing interest and turned it into a lifestyle, awoke in me a passion and a joy that I had never dreamed possible. He taught me how to go deep within myself, how to find my inner strength and power and wrap it around myself like a cloak. Through leather, I found my self.

And yet, as happy as I was being his boy, I wanted more.

Well, not "more," exactly. I could never want more than he could give. I just had a hunger for something different.

It took me a long time to figure out what I wanted, but as soon as I did, I found him: my boy.

He's younger than me, but only by a year. And he's a small one—he's a Gemini, too, and we always look younger than our years. Scott is a full head shorter than me, with tousled blond hair and full lips. He's beautiful, in an ethereal way, and at first I was afraid to handle him too roughly. But I loved taking care of him, buying him trinkets, holding him in my arms on lazy Sunday mornings.

Scott and I started out as vanilla boyfriends. He was fine with me having a Daddy, and even expressed some interest in the scene himself. Excited about the prospect of introducing him to my world, I suggested that he, Howard and I all go out to dinner together.

It seemed like a good idea at the time, but the week leading up to our Friday night engagement was nerve-wracking for me. I wasn't so worried about Scott and Howard liking each other— they were both educated, urbane men with similar politics, and I was sure we'd find something to talk about. No, I was worried about who *I* was going to be around the both of them.

Laugh all you want, but I spent a lot of energy deciding what I was going to wear. See, Daddy likes his boy to be a cute little leather punk. I always wear my combat boots with green laces, raggedy jeans and either a fresh white A-frame or an old T-shirt with some band's name on it. Sometimes I'll spike my hair or throw on a leather vest. When I'm with Daddy I'm brimming with youthful energy, but I'm also paying close attention to him, ready to light his cigarette or fetch him a beer without him having to say a word.

That's a side of me Scott has never seen. When we're together I'm very much a grown-up. While I'm still casual, when we go out in public I'm usually in a freshly ironed shirt, or if I'm feeling particularly preppy a tie and sweater-vest combo. We have a strong intellectual connection, and we're always talking about the latest controversial film screening or art exhibit we've attended.

So I wasn't sure how to behave when I was with the two of them. Should I be Daddy's sharp-tongued scamp or Scott's clean-cut boyfriend? Who should I sit next to? How was I going to serve Daddy without making Scott feel neglected? How was I going to talk to Scott without making Daddy feel ignored?

We had decided on a new Thai place none of us had been to yet in the gayborhood, within walking distance of all of our apartments. The night of our triple date I put on the outfit I had decided on a few days earlier—boots, nice jeans and a plain black T-shirt; respectable enough for Scott, casual enough for Daddy.

I was so nervous that I left the house with half an hour to spare and got to the restaurant fifteen minutes early. A quick glance inside confirmed that there were several empty tables, so I leaned up against the doorjamb and waited. It was a perfect spring night, with a warm breeze and a few clouds scudding across the sky, the smell of rain from the storm a few hours earlier: all my senses were wide awake and my nerves were tingling.

Scott got there first. I recognized his gait from a block away, and noticed with pride the many men that did a double take as he walked past.

"Hi, baby," he said, kissing me on the lips.

"Hey there, good-lookin'." I hugged him close. "Are you nervous?"

"No, why would I be? I'm really excited to meet Howard. Are you nervous?"

"No, no," I lied. I recanted immediately. "Okay, yes, I'm nervous. I'm worried that—I'm just, I don't know, just freaked out a bit, is all, the two of you meeting each other. But I'm sure it will be fine."

"I'm sure too," he said. "You worry too much."

"Yes," a voice boomed from behind him, "he does."

My heart jumped. Daddy was here! I straightened my posture and smiled widely.

"Good evening, Sir!" I said. "This is Scott. Scott, this is my Daddy Howard."

I watched with trepidation as the two most important men in my life shook hands.

"A pleasure," said Scott.

"Same here," said Daddy. "I've heard so much about you."

Scott grinned. "So have I. I especially like that story where you—"

I jumped in before they could make me blush. "Hey, hey, there will be plenty of time to embarrass me over dessert. I'm starving, can we go in already?"

They agreed, laughing, and we ducked inside. The waitress sat us against the window, separated from the rest of the restaurant. Scott and Daddy faced each other, and I sat in between. The three of us ordered beers, and soon the two of them were chatting away like old friends.

The conversation turned to kink over appetizers.

"So," said Daddy, "I've been told that you don't have much experience, am I right?"

Scott swallowed a bite of duck spring roll and nodded. "That's right. I mean, I've always liked it rough"—he winked at me, and I blushed slightly,—"but I don't know anything about, like, official S and M."

"Well, what would you like to know?" asked Daddy.

"I guess I don't have any specific questions, exactly. I learn a lot from the conversations we have," he said, gesturing at me, "but I just want to find out what it's really like. I've read some books, but that's not a substitute."

"No, it's not," said Daddy. He turned to me. "Well, boy,

what's your excuse?"

I choked on my mouthful and started to cough. After a glass of water and a not-so-gentle pounding on the back, I regained my voice. "What do you mean, 'my excuse'?" I asked.

"Come on now, you're hardly a novice. Surely I've taught you enough to give Scotty here a good first scene."

"I, um, well, we don't—I mean, I could, but it's just...you know, our dynamic—"

"Enough. You're babbling." His tone was stern, but there was a smile tugging at the corner of his mouth. I chanced a look at Scott. He was sitting quietly, head cocked, eyes narrowed. I knew that meant he was thinking hard about something.

"Howard," he piped up, "don't give him too hard a time. I'm sure we'll figure *something* out."

Daddy turned his attention to Scott, and a look that I couldn't decipher passed between them.

"All right," he acquiesced, and at just that moment the waitress came to our table with the entrees. Scott started to tell a funny story about one of his clients at work, and soon we were all laughing as I stole bites off of both their plates.

The rest of the meal went smoothly. At one point I had to run to the bathroom. When I got back the two of them were smiling mischievously at each other, but I didn't think too much of it. When the check came Daddy picked it up quietly, and Scott and I thanked him. We left the restaurant and milled about on the corner, debating what to do next.

I pulled out my BlackBerry. "Well, there's Julie's birthday party tonight at Bar Crow, that's not too far from here. Or there's that benefit auction for the gay men's health center uptown. Ooh, or we could go to—"

Daddy cut me off. "No, I don't feel like traipsing all around town."

Scott was nodding. "Yeah. Come on, sweetheart, we go out all the time. Let's take this one night to...get to know each other better."

I looked back and forth between them. "Hey, did you two plot something?"

Daddy was implacable, but Scott winked at me and said, "Maaaaybe."

I knew better than to argue with the both of them. Daddy led the way, and Scott and I tagged along behind, holding hands without speaking. We were almost at his doorstep before I realized where we were going, and I started to get nervous all over again.

When we got inside Daddy sat down in his big chair and gestured at his boots. Without thinking twice I knelt and started unlacing his right one. To my surprise Scott got on his knees next to me and started unlacing Daddy's other boot. *Hmm*, I thought. This could be interesting.

When Daddy's boots were off he leaned forward and grabbed me by the collar of my shirt. He pulled me into a standing position and kissed me hard.

"Tonight," he growled, "that boy is yours. But *you*, boy, are still mine." I nodded silently. Daddy pointed me toward his chair and I sat, my first time on that piece of furniture. Then Scott proceeded to take of my boots. When he started to rub my feet I marveled at the feeling of being serviced. Daddy caressed the back of my neck with his hand while my eyelids drooped with pleasure.

After what felt like long minutes but was probably a few short seconds, Daddy tapped me on the shoulder, indicating that I should stand.

"Look up," said Daddy, pointing at Scott. I got hard at the sight of his big blue eyes staring at us. "Tonight, both of you will travel to a new place inside yourselves. I hope you're ready."

With that pronouncement he grabbed Scott by his upper arm and hauled him into the playroom. Standing him up against the St. Andrew's cross, Daddy shot a look at me. At first I was unsure of what to do, but then I remembered how many of our scenes started, and I lifted Scott's right wrist and put it into the soft leather cuffs already hanging from the bolts in the wood. I tightened the strap. "Too much?" I asked, and he shook his head. I went to the other side and trussed his left wrist and then stood in front of him. Instinct took over and I gripped his hair tight, leaning in for a kiss.

Usually our kisses were sweet and tender, but this time I ravaged his mouth with a passion I'd only ever experienced from the other side, and he let me, opening his lips to my loving assault. He whimpered softly, and I looked down to see his erection tenting his tight jeans. I gave his dick a brief squeeze, then pulled away and went around behind him.

I looked at Daddy and mouthed, *Now what?* He pulled a selection of floggers off the wall behind us and handed me one with thick, soft strands of leather and a stiff, braided handle.

I had never flogged someone before, but I had certainly received my share of whippings. Experience had taught me what felt like a good beating, pain and pleasure interspersed, and what was being delivered by some incompetent striking me as if I were a side of beef. I had even practiced swinging a flogger, many times in fact, and knew that my aim was true. So it was with trepidation and excitement that I took the tool from his hands and draped it over my shoulder.

Daddy moved so that he was standing in front of Scott and began gently playing with his nipples. I knew that Scott's nipples were directly connected to his dick, and the moans and gasps Daddy was achieving told him as much. I began stroking Scott's back, feeling him in a whole new way. I gently palpated his flesh, massaging him, warming up the muscles and reacquainting myself with their position; the way they moved beneath his skin, how my fingerprints stood out red against his pale complexion.

When I judged that he was in a state of relaxation and submission, helped by Daddy's ministrations, I grasped the flogger and began swinging it in a gentle figure eight. I started away from his body and took small steps forward until the tips of the flogger were just barely striking him. His breathing changed slightly, in a way that I recognized as preparation for the sensations to come.

After several minutes of warm-up I started striking him harder, hitting him more with the heavy body of the flogger instead of just the stinging tips. His back began to turn red, and I paid close attention as his muscles tensed and relaxed, as his breath moved in and out of his body. Daddy was paying attention too, stroking his chest, playing with his nipples, sometimes kissing him or biting at his lips. More than a few times I caught Daddy's eye as I worked, and I felt a jolt of electricity between us and knew that Scott was the conduit of that energy.

I've asked tops before what they get out of a flogging and never received an answer to my satisfaction. But as I got more and more involved, felt the rhythm of my arm and shoulder steady, grew hypnotized by the steady beat of leather against flesh, I began to understand. Watching Scott's body respond to me was an unspoken kind of conversation, and I fell in love with him in a whole new way. I was telling, or rather showing him, how much he could experience, all the different ways his body could process feelings. I heard him gasp and sometimes cry out; I could see his shoulders rise and fall as he took deep, cleansing breaths.

I didn't get an erection, but I was opening up, physically and emotionally, in a new way. I had never identified as dominant before and never felt like a top, but as I flogged Scott I found myself telling him to take it for me, to take the pain I was giving him and give it back to me. Daddy caught my eye and gave me an encouraging smile, obviously reminded of all the times he had told me the same things.

Talking to Scott that way showed me what I had been missing. I was a boy, yes, and a good one, but there was also a Daddy in me, a man who wanted to hurt but also comfort, who wanted to bring a boy to tears and then lick them away. I felt strong, powerful, yet also honored that this beautiful, brilliant man was giving this gift to me, was letting me take control of him and trusting me to give back that power.

Alas, my stint as a top was coming to a close. A novice bottom, Scott seemed to have a hard time relaxing, and his breath was coming in short, sharp gasps that were edging into sobs. I slowed and then stopped and went up to him, putting my hands gently on his back, feeling the warmth and grinning despite myself at the beautiful swollen flesh that I had created.

"You okay, baby?" I whispered.

He nodded slowly. Scott was never one to skimp on words so I knew he must have gone deep inside himself, into that place where bottoms go when we're taken into a submissive state of mind. Daddy moved away and beckoned me to come around to the front of the cross. When I did I saw tear tracks down my younger boyfriend's cheeks and a soft smile on his face.

I leaned in and kissed him gently. He looked at me trustingly as I took his hands out of the restraints, and when I was done he spontaneously went down on his knees and kissed my feet. Daddy started massaging my shoulders and I leaned back into his hands.

"Now, boy," he rumbled in my ear, "what would you like to learn next?"

POP TINGLE

David Holly

My parents were evangelical Christians, so when I wrote a paper questioning the authenticity of the Bible for my high school English class, all hell broke loose. I never expected my father to see my paper, but he sneaked it from my laptop, read it and blew his stack. He stormed around for ten minutes, belted me twice and cast me out of the house with only the clothes I was wearing. Behind him stood my mother, praying for my eternal damnation.

I thought then that it was the worst night of my life, but I soon found out that worse were coming. I slept on a friend's couch for a couple of months, until his parents claimed that they could not support me further. I tried calling home, but my mother hung up when she heard my voice. That night I slept on a bench in the Park Blocks, which turned out to be some wine guzzler's favorite bench. His psycho friends roughed me up and would have robbed me if I'd had anything to steal.

Two months away from graduating high school, I stopped going altogether. Surviving the streets was too hard to include

academics. My education was different from that of my class-
mates. I learned how to eat garbage, sleep in doorways, beg
for money and run con games on tourists. Edible food can be
found in Dumpsters and people toss out all kinds of cool stuff.
I learned how to panhandle too, though I was never as good as
others.

I'd been living on the street for almost a year when I met Pop
Tingle. I was squatting in the stairwell of an unkempt parking
garage with about fifty other kids ranging in age from twelve to
twenty-nine. We'd fixed up the stairwell, even hauling in cast-
off furniture so the landings were homey.

I'd spent a hard evening panhandling. After raking in four
bucks, I was dragging my hungry ass back to the parking garage
when an older dude sitting at a sidewalk café beckoned me.

"I'm not doing anything," I yelped before he could accuse me
of stealing his shit.

Smiling, he gestured toward an untouched piece of cheesecake covered with a chocolate sauce. "What would you do for
this?" he taunted.

"What do you want?" I asked. I lusted after that cheesecake,
but the streets had taught me the ways of older dudes. Their
malevolent tactics entailed barebacking a boy's ass, shooting
him full of diseased cum and kicking him out before the wife
got home. Many of the kids sold their asses and got infected for
their trouble, but I'd kept mine intact.

This guy acted as if my natural caution was a malady. "You're
a suspicious bugger, aren't you?"

"I got good reason," I said. Lots of men had wanted to use
me—plenty of women too. "Let me take a few pictures," they'd
say, offering pizza in trade, sometimes dope or booze. I kept
refusing. The payment could not be worth what I would endure.
I'd seen too many young kids die, their eyes wild with terror.

I started to walk away, but the man called me again. "What's your name?" he asked, holding out the plate. I drooled onto my decrepit sneakers.

"Eric," I said.

"No," he said, withdrawing the plate.

"Shit." I didn't want to waste more time on this asshole.

His eyes glinted with weird amusement, a kitty toying with a mouse. "No, Eric isn't your name."

"It sure as hell is."

"Your name is Bottom."

Turning on my heel, I gave my parting shot: "You're fuckin' nuts."

His words were honeyed as he enticed me back. "Say your name is Bottom. Say it and you can eat it."

"You're crazier than shit."

"Tell me that your name is Bottom. Say it, and this whole piece of delicious cheesecake is all yours."

"All right, my goddamn name is fuckin' Bottom." Pausing, I added, "Nick Bottom the Weaver."

"So you're literate? Good boy, Bottom." He pushed the plate across the table. I grabbed for it, but he kept hold of the plate. "In the civilized world, we sit at the table to eat our dessert. Sit, Bottom."

I sat down, and he pulled his hand away. I picked up the fork and dug into the cheesecake. He didn't say anything while I gobbled down the dessert. When I finished, I stood up fast. "I gotta get going."

He waved his hand. "Make sure you brush your teeth, Bottom."

"Like there's a toothbrush and a sink in the stairwell," I sneered. "Fuckin' nuts."

* * *

The next afternoon my friend Skeet and I were running a bus ticket scam near Pioneer Courthouse Square. We begged used tickets from people getting off the bus and then sold them at reduced rates to tourists. Tourists were so preoccupied with their own shit that they usually didn't notice that the tickets had expired.

Two local real estate brokers had just told me to get a job when I noticed the old cheesecake dude. He carried an untouched fast-food bag, which he held out invitingly.

"Is that for me?"

"What's your name?"

"Bottom," I said quickly.

"Not enough. Show me that you're a sissy."

"Huh?"

He waved the bag until I drooled. "Show everyone that you're a sissy. If you walk like a girl up the length of the platform, you can have the bag."

"I don't know how."

"Wiggle it," he ordered.

"Huh?"

"Wiggle your sexy butt."

"Shit."

He opened the bag, and the heady aroma of a burger and fries wafted out. "There's a chocolate milkshake too," he said. "All for something so simple."

I gave my ass a little shake as I took a couple of steps, but that wasn't enough for him. "No, wiggle it like you mean it. Walk down the platform. Wiggle your ass hard enough and long enough to attract attention. I want to see eyes turning in your direction."

"Go for it, dude," Skeet urged. "I'd shake my booty for that bag."

Hesitating no longer, I wiggled my ass for all it was worth. The cheesecake dude wasn't satisfied until I had every eye turned upon me. I tried so hard that I nearly fell over, but I wasn't walking like any girl. With a contemptuous remark about my performance, he handed me the bag and departed.

My crowd had enjoyed my humiliation, so I started panhandling. My hat was filled with dollar bills within a few minutes. Word must have gotten around because I kept raking in cash all day.

I awoke disoriented. For a few seconds I thought that I was safe at home in my own bed. The white walls betrayed themselves, as did the white hospital bed. My lower back burned, as did my upper arm. I climbed out of the bed to give my body a quick survey. I was wearing white thong underwear with little purple dots. A bandage covered my lower back and another wrapped my right bicep. I rushed to the toilet and lowered the thong underwear. My pubic hair was gone. My cock and balls were okay, but I had been shaved. So had my legs. Urgency claimed me. I pissed, washed my hands, sipped some water and turned toward the full-length mirror. I didn't even recognize myself. Every hair on my body had been shaved—even my head was bald.

"Shit," I yelped as memories flooded back.

Walking back to the parking structure after my profitable panhandling experience, I noticed a black limousine beside the curb, its driver lounging in the shadows. I'd heard plenty about shit like that. A homeless kid gets in the car and is never seen again. Maybe in a couple of months the authorities find his gang-raped body. I turned to flee.

"Hey, Bottom. How'd you like the burger and fries? Did that shake taste good?"

"What do you want?" I asked, neither fleeing nor approaching.

He stepped out into the glare of the streetlights. He didn't look threatening. "Pop Tingle likes the way you obeyed him."

That made me curious. I took a closer look at the guy. He was in his early thirties, a creamy-skinned mix of African American and red-haired Nordic ancestry with a hint of Asian tossed into the melting pot. He had a gym-sculpted body with natural attributes. Abruptly he smiled, which emboldened me to ask who he was.

"You can call me Mr. Jack. I'm Pop Tingle's assistant."

"Who the fuck is Pop Tingle?"

"The best pop you'll ever have, Bottom."

It didn't take five minutes for Mr. Jack to talk me into the car. I sat beside him as we slid through the darkening streets. Mr. Jack described the delights of Pop Tingle's home: great food, warm beds, gigantic televisions, gym memberships. "But first," Mr. Jack said, "you need a medical checkup. After living on the streets, your health could be compromised."

The clinic was closed for the night, but Doctor Tartt met us at the back door. Mr. Jack slipped her an envelope and escorted me into an examination room. A male nurse came in, introduced himself, weighed me; took my temperature, pulse and blood pressure and handed me a hospital gown. "Take everything off," the nurse, Armando, said. "The examination will be thorough."

I stripped naked, and Armando helped me into the gown. Then he started filling a hypodermic. "What the fuck's that?" I gasped.

"Just a shot. You're a little nervous. This will help relax you."

I didn't like the idea, but Armando stuck my arm before I

could protest. A feeling of euphoria came over me before he pulled the needle out.

Doctor Tartt came in and examined me. I didn't care when they took away the hospital gown, along with my street clothes. I giggled as they gave me a series of enemas, and I laughed as they shaved me head to toe. Mr. Jack and Armando scrubbed me under the shower before the tattoo artist arrived. I was dozing facedown on the examination table when he began to work on me. I was dimly aware of the needle for a while.

Now, standing in front of the mirror with nothing covering my body but a few bandages and a printed thong, I tried to remember if anything else had been done to me. I was still standing when Doctor Tartt and Armando entered. Both smiled brightly at me, but Mr. Jack slipped in behind them and watched me closely.

"Are you ready to see your body art?" Doctor Tartt asked brightly.

I nodded, so she removed the bandage from my arm. A band of gay rainbow shapes encircled my arm. I slipped into a state of shock so profound that I lost all willpower.

"It's beautiful," Armando gasped. "What a wonderful way to come out to everyone."

"Let's see your back," Doctor Tartt said, carefully pulling off the bandage.

Intricate designs of flowers arose from my buttcrack and swelled to cover my lower back. The floral design surrounded ornate calligraphy that spelled *Bottom*. Marked for life with that tramp stamp, I stood naked, hairless and cruelly exposed.

"So pretty," Armando said, and I turned my dull, dazed eyes upon him.

"Time to get dressed, Bottom," Mr. Jack said. I nodded numbly. He handed me a slinky crop top and a pair of Lycra shorts. After tucking my thong between my buttocks, I pulled on the top, which did not descend to my navel, and I pulled up the shorts, which my ass packed effeminately. A pair of pink sneakers completed this ensemble. With my shaved head and my fuck-my-ass clothing, my own mother would have passed me in the street.

Pop Tingle owned one of those Nob Hill mansions that hung over the rocky cliff. The house had a four-car garage built into one side of the house, while the other wing enclosed a swimming pool. The front entrance was carved wood in a twining rose pattern. When Mr. Jack escorted me through the front hall into the room with the curving staircase, Pop Tingle came in from the pool. He was wearing lime swim briefs, and I gulped at the sight.

"You've sure taken care of yourself," I said. Not only was Pop Tingle well-muscled with a defined chest, rippling abdominals and powerful buttocks, but he had a thick cock, which his thin swimsuit did nothing to conceal.

Mr. Jack grinned at my surprise while Pop Tingle inspected me from head to toe. "You were right about his ass, Pop Tingle," Mr. Jack said. "The new Bottom packs his shorts."

Pop Tingle's cock was stirring in his swimsuit. I watched with fascination as it lengthened and stretched the fabric. "Bring the anal lube, Jack-Off."

Mr. Jack rushed from the room. Pop Tingle's cock was getting harder. He pulled off his swimsuit so I could watch his dick engorge. At that moment, I realized two things. First, Mr. Jack was the old Bottom who had graduated to jack-off servant, and the new Bottom, me, was about to get his ass fucked. For some reason, I accepted the situation. When Pop Tingle ran his hands over my ass, feeling me up outrageously, I didn't protest.

His lips brushed my ear. "Do you know why I picked you, Bottom?" he asked.

I knew. At times my bountiful bubblebutt had been the bane of my existence. I got teased about it while I was still in high school, and I'd had hundreds of offers for it while I was living on the street. The other boys had told me I had a good thing going if I only had enough sense to use it. Of course, those same boys had no sense themselves. They were taking street drugs, even drugs to grow their breasts and make themselves more girlish. The chemicals those kids poured into their bodies would have given everybody in China a howling harelip, but they made their money by pleasing men who wanted ladyboys. I'd seen fourteen-year-old boys with budding boobs and shrunken testicles.

Pop Tingle was undressing me. He removed my sneakers, then pulled down my shorts. "Cute," he commented, fingering my thong. "I'll tell Jack-Off that you'll be wearing thong underwear exclusively. Your swimsuits too." He kissed my ass just below my tramp stamp. By then, Mr. Jack was back with the anal lube. Pop Tingle pulled down my underwear. Leaving my crop top in place, he ordered me to climb onto the couch and lean over the back.

Wondering why I was obeying him, I dropped onto the couch, pressed my knees into the cushions and leaned over the back. My heart was thundering. I had never been fucked, not in all my time on the street.

Pop Tingle didn't mount me right away. He rubbed his hands over my butt, caressing, squeezing and moving ever closer to my crack. "I'm going to make you a bottom," he whispered in my ear. "Right now, you don't know what you are. I will teach you. I will be a father to you, and I will remake you in the image I desire."

A feeling of such safety came over me that I relaxed utterly. I felt like I had been holding my breath since the night my parents threw me away, and my terrors expelled in one puff. "Yes, Bottom, I'll take care of you. I may be a demanding father, but I promise to protect you and keep you well—providing that you give yourself to me unreservedly."

His lubricated finger touched my asshole. I felt hot all over. Pop Tingle loved me, and he would take care of me. "I'm yours," I breathed, and his finger twisted my asshole and slipped pleasantly into me.

"Good choice, Bottom," Mr. Jack said. Standing before my eyes while Pop Tingle finger-fucked my ass, Mr. Jack dropped his shirt on floor. He showed me the pride tattoo on his bicep. Then he pulled off his shoes and tight trousers, so I could see his golden thong underwear and the fuck-me tramp stamp on his lower back.

Pop Tingle pulled his finger out of my ass and positioned himself between my spread calves. I could feel his thick cock pressing against my buttcrack. "Push your ass back, Bottom, and draw a deep breath. That's it. Let it out. Another deep breath and push hard with your asshole. Push like you're trying to push something out."

A rush of panic swept over me. Pop Tingle slapped my ass. "No, don't tighten your sphincter. You're not getting off this couch until you have my cum in your ass."

At that news, my facial expression must have been comical, because Mr. Jack chortled as he placed a towel on a chair, pulled down his thong, and sat to beat his meat while he watched me.

"You're Pop Tingle's new fuck toy, Bottom," Mr. Jack said. He spit into his hand and started jerking off.

Mr. Jack had drawn my attention for a second, long enough for Pop Tingle to place the head of his cock against my asshole. I felt a tremendous pressure in my ass. "You're a bottom," Pop

Tingle breathed in my ear. "Bottoms take it up the ass. Deep breaths. Push. Good. Now you're taking it."

Pop Tingle pushed deep into me, pulled back, and thrust deeper. My mind was in a whirl. I was doing the very thing I'd vowed I would never do. What's more, I was starting to like it. Warm, pleasant feelings swept through me. My cock had been soft, but it hardened as Pop Tingle fucked me and whispered strange suggestions into my ear. He told me that I was a gay boy, a queer, a faggot, a sodomite. None of those words sounded bad when he said them. When Pop Tingle told me that I was a fag, it rang of reassurance rather than censure.

Mr. Jack was spanking his monkey feverishly while he sat witness to my anal initiation. He stroked his shaft and toyed with his dickhead.

"This is it, Bottom," Pop Tingle whispered. His breath was husky in my ear. I could feel the heat from his trembling body. "This is it. I'm going to come in your ass." He emitted a long, low moan. I had thought that I would feel the cum shooting into me, but I didn't. What I felt was a sense of peace. Hunched over the couch with Pop Tingle shooting his spunk into my ass while Mr. Jack jerked his cock and shot his load into the towel, I felt safe and secure. A sense of love and belonging swept over me.

"I love you, Pop Tingle," I said simply.

In answer, Pop Tingle reached under the couch cushion and pulled out a thick butt plug that had been concealed there. "When I pull my cock out, hold your sphincter tight. Don't let my cum leak out. I'm going to wipe your asscrack. Then I'm going to insert this plug. A tight thong will keep the plug from popping out. We'll leave it in you for a couple of hours, long enough for your body to absorb my cum. Then I will be a part of you, just as I am a part of Jack-Off."

Pop Tingle did exactly as he said. The butt plug was wider

than his cock and I thought that it would split me going in. However, I took it okay. The plain green thong was painfully tight up my crack, so even though my ass worked the butt plug, I couldn't squeeze it out. Walking around was a weird experience with that tremendous load up my ass, but after a while I got used to it.

Mr. Jack and I were sunning naked by the swimming pool one afternoon in early June when he started asking me about my former life. In the three months I had been with Mr. Jack and Pop Tingle we had found out a few things about each other, but our lives together were separate from anything else we had experienced. Of course, I knew Mr. Jack's real name and he knew mine, but Pop Tingle insisted that we call each other by the names he assigned. I even knew Pop Tingle's real name— after all, the mail was delivered to the house, and Mr. Jack and I used credit cards with Pop Tingle's identity stamped on them during our frequent shopping trips.

I told him about why my parents threw me out and about my life on the streets.

"Dad ordered me out after he caught me sucking my friend Tim's cock," Mr. Jack said. "I tried selling blow jobs on Eighty-Second Avenue and got arrested. A guy who produced gay porn bailed me out. I've acted in hundreds of films, and the web's loaded with pictures of me sucking cocks. I was lucky. Lots of those kids got sick right away, but I never took it up the ass until I met Pop Tingle."

We talked about how he met Pop Tingle and his fifteen years as Bottom. "Now it's your turn, Bottom," he said.

"You think that someday I'll be helping recruit my replacement?"

"I guess it depends. In fifteen years, Pop Tingle will be sixty-seven. I guess he could still be going strong at that age."

"Will you be around, Mr. Jack?"

"Of course I will, Bottom. It's a lifetime career with Pop Tingle. He takes care of us. And just in case something happens to him, he's set up a trust fund for me. I'm set for life, and he'll do the same for you eventually—after you prove your loyalty."

"Prove my loyalty? I've done everything he wants. Everything. Yesterday he stuck a vibrator up my ass and worked the remote control settings. For half the day, he kept moving it from low hum to super throb."

Mr. Jack laughed at the description. "Pop Tingle loves playing with us. Did he make you come?"

"I had some cum oozing out of my cock, but I didn't have an orgasm. It still felt good, but I like it better when he fucks me with his cock."

"Yeah, you're a natural fuck toy. It took me a while before I learned to like doing anal. I'm a natural cocksucker."

My cock was hard by then, so I rolled over. Mr. Jack looked at my erection and grinned. "I wish that I could suck it. I'm going to ask Pop Tingle if I can suck you while he fucks you."

Pop Tingle had strict rules against Mr. Jack and me coming without him being present. He had me on a strict anal regimen, so I was not allowed any genital stimulation without a cock or sex toy up my ass. After the first few butt fucks, he had encouraged me to jerk off while he was fucking me, but that was all I had been allowed up until then.

"Do you think he'll go for it?'

"Probably. That's enough tanning for today. Let's shower and get dressed. We need to go shopping. Pop Tingle wants you dressed as a schoolgirl in a short skirt for tonight's party."

"I'd like to see some of the movies you starred in," I said as we walked naked into the house.

"We'll ask Pop Tingle. He has the complete collection. Wait a minute, Bottom; that's wrong. Don't walk all open. Pretend that you don't have a cock. Walk in a straight line with one foot in front of the other as you step."

"Like this?" I asked.

"Yes, but cross your legs over a little more. Stand up straight. Shoulders back. Sway your hips and walk gracefully. Try to glide and look confident. That's it."

"This takes concentration."

"After a few years, you'll forget you ever walked any other way."

More than a year elapsed before Pop Tingle showed *Swim Slurp*, one of Mr. Jack's movies. The cold January night we watched it, Pop Tingle made Mr. Jack and me wear vibrating butt plugs. In addition to these accessories, Mr. Jack was dressed in whisper-thin spandex while I wore a cheerleader outfit with a skirt so short it barely covered my butt. After we watched a young Mr. Jack suck off the whole swim team, Pop Tingle ordered Mr. Jack to suck my dick. That was the first time. Excited, I sat in my chair with the vibrating plug up my ass, with Pop Tingle working the controls, while Mr. Jack blew me. I lolled back, relishing the vibrating fullness in my ass as the waves of pleasure grew in my dickhead. Raptures followed as my semen gushed. Mr. Jack's throat was working as he took my cum. When he finished, he scrubbed my cock and balls with a warm washrag.

Pop Tingle was sitting in his chair, fondling his cock and working the controls of my vibrator. "Don't start thinking you're a top because you got a blow job, Bottom," he ordered. "You're a receiver, not a penetrator."

Grinning, I stood and bent forward so my skirt pulled up

over my ass and showed off the plug in my ass. "I could never be a top, Pop Tingle. I wish that you'd fuck my ass right now."

"Jack-Off, pull that plug out of Bottom's asshole."

Mr. Jack hastened to comply. Pop Tingle put the remote control aside and came close behind me. "Let's pretend we're going to play leap frog, Bottom. You bend, and I'll jump over you."

I assumed the position, joyfully aware that he wasn't about to jump over me. "Keep your legs closer together," Pop Tingle ordered.

His cock was positioned a little above my asshole, so when he inserted his cock I gasped with surprise. "Keep your legs closer together, Bottom," Pop Tingle ordered.

"Won't that hurt?"

Mr. Jack rushed to reassure me. "Pop Tingle and I call it the Flying Doggie, but some gay guys say it's Leap Frog," Mr. Jack contributed. "In this position, keeping your legs shut slackens your anus, which is important because Pop Tingle's angle will be downward—good for you because his cock will kindle special parts of your rectum and asshole."

"Thanks for the lecture, professor," I quipped, which made even Pop Tingle snicker.

Pop Tingle took me in the flying doggie position. Mounting my back, he drove his cock downward. When his dickhead hit my prostate, I felt a burst of sexual thrills so intense that I nearly came. Had I not just shot my load into Mr. Jack's mouth, I would surely have gotten my rocks off.

Mr. Jack smirked as Pop Tingle worked his cock in my ass. He lubed his hand and started pounding his shaft and thumbing his dickhead. Abruptly, Pop Tingle saw what Mr. Jack was doing.

"Stop that, Jack-Off. Stop it now." Pop Tingle continued

humping me while he admonished Mr. Jack. "Did I give your permission to beat your meat, Jack-Off?"

I craned my neck in order to view Mr. Jack's face. He looked so crestfallen that I giggled.

"Uh, no, Pop Tingle. I just thought..."

Pop Tingle was giving me a slow, comfortable butt fuck. He did not vary his stroke in the least as he said, "Don't think, Jack-Off. And never jerk your cock until I order you to jerk it."

My cock was hard again. Little tingles sparked in the head of it. Pop Tingle maintained his slow rhythm, pulling back until the head of his cock swelled my asshole and then pushing forward until he buried his whole shaft. Every stroke hit my prostate most deliciously. My dick grew heavier; I would come soon. To my disappointment, Pop Tingle got off first. He emitted a keening moan that turned into howled words: "Oh, Bottom. Your ass is so good. Oh, you sissy. Here I come, Bottom. I'm shooting cum into your ass."

Pop Tingle pulled his cock out before I could come. I had been so close. I bit my lip, forbidding myself to speak. How could I complain about one missed orgasm when he had been so good to me? He took care of me, and all he demanded was my devotion, obedience and submission. Counting that night, he'd deposited his cum in my ass one hundred and forty-nine times. I knew the number because Pop Tingle required that I keep a diary. Every day I wrote an explicit account of my sexual adventures, the sissified clothes I had worn, time spent tanning or exercising at the gym and other assorted tasks such as doctor and dental appointments and shopping trips with Mr. Jack.

"I have a treat for you, Bottom. And one for Jack-Off, too. You're going to blow him."

"Bottom is going to suck my dick?" Mr. Jack purred.

"Yes, Jack-Off."

I blanched. I'd never taken Pop Tingle's—or anyone else's—cock in my mouth. "I've never done that," I managed.

"Time to learn, Bottom," Pop Tingle said. "How can you be a successful sissy if you don't swallow cum?"

Mr. Jack sat on the couch, and to my dismay, his cock hardened instantly. "Touch your lips to the head, Bottom. Kiss it."

My heart thundering, I did as Pop Tingle ordered. I kissed the head of Mr. Jack's dick and was surprised by the smoothness of his skin. His dick had a pleasant tangy taste. I had a dark suspicion regarding the substance I was savoring, but it didn't taste bad. Truth to tell, it pleased my taste buds. I licked his dick head, letting the head slip over my lips and into my mouth.

"Go down on him, Bottom," Pop Tingle ordered. "Let his cock slide along your tongue. You're going to like it."

I lifted my head. "How does he know I'm going to like it?" After all, Pop Tingle was a top, through and through. What cocksucking experience could he have? None!

"Take it into your mouth, Bottom," Mr. Jack whispered. "You will like it. You're a natural sissy. All sissies like to suck cock. You'll see."

"Suck him, Bottom," Pop Tingle ordered.

I let Mr. Jack's cock slide along my tongue. I pulled my head back and went down again. His cock was filling my mouth. I teased his cock with my lips, then I licked down the shaft. I was in ecstasy.

"You'll suck Jack-Off until he comes, Bottom," Pop Tingle said. "You're going to swallow his cum. Meanwhile, I'll be giving you your present. He held an elegant wooden gift box, which he opened to reveal a golden prostate massager. The gold-plated massager did not vibrate but had fluid curves, and it was the smoothest metal I'd ever felt. Pop Tingle warmed it between his hands, and then he coated it with a thick lubricant.

I slid my lips over Mr. Jack's dick while Pop Tingle inserted his finger through the massager's ringed end and slid it into my ass. Delicious feelings swept over me. I went down hard on Mr. Jack, sucking him ravenously. Pop Tingle slowly worked the massager inside of me. My body was a rapture of sensation. I felt Mr. Jack's cock slacken for three seconds before it stiffened to supreme hardness. As I worried the head with my lips, it twitched. A hot tasty fluid covered my tongue. I swallowed it down while deep pleasure sensations filled my ass. My cock was not fully hard, but it was dripping cum. Delirious pleasure swept over me. More cum was in my mouth and I savored it before I swallowed. Meanwhile Pop Tingle kept massaging me with the golden tool, driving me to pinnacles of sexual rapture that were beyond imagining.

Shortly after that day, I became aware of how much I'd changed. I'd been a good student in high school with all that implies: conformist, mundane, lackadaisical and ordinary. While I lived on the street I hadn't read serious works, nor had I exercised my brain much. Pop Tingle gave me the leisure for study. He owned an impressive library, and one day I picked up a copy of *Emerson's Essays*. I struggled through "Self-Reliance" until I had a fair idea what Emerson meant. I dipped into Thoreau, enjoying *Walden* and coming alive with "Civil Disobedience."

For the next six months I read my way through the greatest American authors, the profound and the downright fun. Meanwhile, Mr. Jack watched old movies. I watched classic films with him, but mostly I read. I moved into British literature, philosophy, history and religious studies.

In August of my second year since my rebirth as Bottom, the three of us were sunning at Rooster Rock, a legal state-operated nude beach. In spite of our sunscreen, we three had tanned nicely that summer. My tattoos had taken on a special glow. I was hotly aware of the leers I collected from the numerous gay men who enjoyed the ambiance, but never did I consider any disloyalty toward Pop Tingle.

Emerging naked from the river, I strutted to our beach blanket and sprawled facedown between Pop Tingle and Mr. Jack. "Don't burn your cock, Pop Tingle," I warned.

"Never fear, Bottom. I'm looking forward to planting it in your ass tonight."

"I'm looking forward to that too," I agreed.

"I miss those days," Mr. Jack said. "I miss your cock in my ass."

"I fucked you silly just last week, Jack-Off," Pop Tingle remonstrated, "while Bottom blew you."

Mr. Jack giggled. "Bottom and I were doing the nine and sixty, Pop Tingle. We were both sucking cock while you fucked my ass."

"I know. I read Bottom's diary. Our Bottom has a promising future as a writer. He certainly has become well read lately. What are you reading now, Bottom?"

The sun was making my ass hot, so I rolled over, rubbing my bare buttocks against Pop Tingle as I did so. "I just read your entire ten-volume set of *The Golden Bough*. It really puts religion in context. I'm understanding literature in ways I never did before. The paintings in the art museum too."

I felt as if the sun had grown much hotter. It was burning into my brain. I sat up, and the beach was bathed in a golden glow. Naked men of all shapes and sizes cruised under the summer sun. The men outnumbered the women, just as gay people outnumbered the breeders. Enlightenment struck me. In submitting to Pop Tingle, I had found a perfect freedom. I was not bound to a life of wife, job and children. I had recaptured

Eden. I was having the best sex imaginable, and in between I could exercise both body and brain. My spirit swelled. I realized then just how deeply I loved Pop Tingle, and Mr. Jack too. I had rejected my parents' cosmic viewpoint, and after passing through a homeless nightmare, I had awakened into a peace that their cramped mentalities could never understand.

MARKEY

Mark Wildyr

"Take the shot," I whispered as the four-point buck left the cover of the pine forest and hesitantly stepped onto the narrow meadow. The animal took a long look around before carefully lowering his head to the pale autumn grass.

"Me!" Markey gasped aloud. The white tail's head shot up, ears flicking nervously. The animals were skittish as hell this late in the season. We had glimpsed a button buck and a spike, both of which were legal, but this was our first decent shot of the hunt.

"Yes, you!" I hissed. "Take it." For someone who had been so blessed eager to come on the hunt, Marcus Markey seemed downright reluctant to pull the trigger. "Markey, point that fucking rifle and shoot." I allowed a little exasperation to seep into my voice, knowing that would motivate him.

He eased the Remington thirty-aught-six over the edge of the blind and took a bead. I watched as he drew a breath, held it and squeezed. Judging from the stricken look on his face as the report echoed against the far hills, his aim had been good. The second last thing the kid desired was to kill a living animal; the *very* last thing was to look like a pussy to someone he looked up to...and that would be me.

There was a gulp and the strangled words, "Got him."

"Good shot, buddy. Your first kill."

"Yeah...kill," he responded with another gulp.

"Well, let's go collect him," I said, leaving the blind and starting down the hill.

I had recently returned to my Oklahoma hometown of Victor for the first time in fifteen, tumultuous years. If the navy had tamed my wild side, the SEALS handed it back in spades. You won't have read or heard news reports about the clandestine missions I'd been on, but I have killed and collected commendations for the killing. Quiet heroes, the SecNav once said of my team.

I would likely have finished out my career and retired to a restless pastoral life of secret memories had it not been for Beet. When Beet—Warren Borak—a lithe, dangerous man four years my senior, took a nineteen-year-old tadpole under his wing, neither of us suspected powerful forces had been unleashed. He guided me, counseled me, nurtured me and protected me. And one memorable, moonless night in Lebanon, he fucked me vigorously in the excitement of an especially brutal action while we waited for the team to reassemble.

My life was never the same after that. Nor was my future... our future. Ten years into my enlistment, Beet and I got drunk with some buddies in Naples and our physical attraction for one another surfaced. We were kicked out of the navy in record time and with as little fanfare as possible.

We became mercenaries, fighting for causes just and not-so-just all over Africa and Southeast Asia. Happy and open about our relationship, we dared the macho world of mercenaries to do something about it, but those intrepid warriors didn't give a shit. So we hired out for buckets full of money to do what our government had trained us to do for peanuts.

Then last year, my beautiful Beet...a nickname hung on him by the SEALS...died in a firefight with a vicious gang in Africa. That he, a superbly trained professional, should die at the hands of rank amateurs strung out on local drugs was almost beyond belief. I completed my contract, taking a terrible toll on the tribal militia that had killed my beloved. Collecting my own pay and a whopping life insurance settlement as Beet's beneficiary, I returned to the United States and tarried in the East until it was clear Uncle Sam had no beef with me for my activities of the last five years. Then I returned home.

Marcus Markey was an eight-year-old neighbor kid when I left for boot camp at Grand Island Naval Training Station. The boy had lived next door to us since the family returned to Victor upon the death of his GI father in Kosovo. Markey, who had adopted me as his big brother, struggled beside me with all the push-ups, sit-ups, pull-ups, dips, flutter kicks, running and swimming I did for a month to get ready for boot. He even attempted the Ninjutsu and Israeli Krav Maga moves recommended by the BUD/S—that would be the Basic Underwater Demolition/SEAL training—website. After each workout, he liked to run his hands over my sweaty biceps to test the hard muscle; it bothered me in a vague way I didn't understand back then. Markey went to the bus station with my family to see me off, and I still recall his thin arms locked around my waist in a good-bye hug, and the tears that soaked my shirt.

Now, glancing at him as we strode down the meadow, I could still see traces of that shy, adoring kid in this lanky twenty-three-year-old. He'd retained the creamy complexion and black sloe-eyes that gave him a slightly foreign cast. A once shaggy mop of black hair was cut short in a vaguely military style. But if Markey ever joined up, he was in for a bad time until he got tough enough to secure his own ground. It wasn't just that he was far beyond merely handsome; his long, curled lashes alone would earn him grief in the barracks. Markey could have been a beautiful girl except for the Adam's apple. I wondered if he had ever cross-dressed. There wasn't a sign of a beard on his smooth skin, although I'm sure there was one; it merely cleaned up well. There wasn't much of the kid I knew fifteen years ago in this fantastic youth—except for the shy, diffident demeanor.

"Kinda small," he observed wryly as we reached the fallen stag.

"It'll make good venison. Well, let's get at it," I suggested, noting the absence of any pride in the kill. "We've gotta field dress him."

"You mean cut him up?" The words were almost strangled.

"You want to leave him for the coyotes?"

"N-no. Of course not. But I don't know how."

"We'll gut him now and pack him back to camp to dry out a little."

"Uh...okay. Will he be all right tonight? You know, he won't go bad?"

"No. It's cool enough. He'll hold for a couple of days."

We hauled the buck away from the kill area and strung him up in a tree. After a couple of false starts, Markey slit its belly with a grimace of distaste. When that job was done, we hauled the carcass back to camp where we hung it again, washed out the cavity, and left it to dry. Then I grabbed a bar of soap, stripped, and waded into the lake. Ignoring the shock of cold water, I lathered up while Markey stood on the shore staring at me in disbelief. After all, it *was* November.

"If I've learned one thing in the last ten years, it's to keep clean," I called. "Keeping clean is half of staying healthy. Coming in?"

I watched as he undressed in the late afternoon sun, revealing a long-limbed, clean-muscled physique with unblemished skin and little body hair except for a pubic bush. Visibly embarrassed, he turned with his flank toward me, which merely silhouetted a long cock sprouting from curly hair. He rushed into the water and gasped aloud at its frigid grip.

I continued lathering, well aware of black eyes studying me closely. I rinsed and repeated the process until my skin squeaked. When I tossed him the soap, he seemed frozen in place. Then he floundered frantically until he recovered the bar. As Markey scrubbed, I could tell my inspection bothered him, so I swam out into the lake. Sufficiently warmed by my exertions, I silently submerged and covered the distance to the shore underwater. When I surfaced beside him, Markey was frantically calling my name.

"Right here," I said quietly, startling him.

"Damn, Daniel! I thought something happened to you. You were under for a long time."

"A fifty-yard underwater swim is mandatory for SEALS." I laughed. "You'd be surprised how many tadpoles had to have water pumped out of their lungs after their first try."

Markey's teeth were chattering, so I crawled out of the water, knowing he would follow. To spare him further embarrassment, I kept my eyes averted as we dried off and dressed. I did the cooking, a trade-off for him cleaning up the gear afterward. Later, as darkness was wresting supremacy from light, we sat at a campfire and sucked on long-necked bottles of beer.

"How was it?" he asked out of the blue. "You know, the SEALS."

"Great! Best time of my life."

"Why'd you get out?"

I swallowed the temptation to tell him the truth. "Found out there was more money to be made outside the navy for doing the same thing."

"I heard you were a soldier of fortune, but I didn't believe it."

"Why not?"

"You were so gung-ho."

"You grow out of that pretty quick."

He let a small silence grow as I sensed some of the hero worship leaking away. Then, "How come you went for the SEALS?"

"After boot, I got caught up in the spirit and put in for BUD/S training."

"How was it?"

"Hell," I said simply.

He grinned into the dying flames. "How about Hell Week?"

"Hell on steroids. You thinking about becoming a tadpole?"

That brought a quick frown and another swig from the bottle. "Naw. Not cut out for it. Wouldn't fit in," he added enigmatically.

I left it where it was, and we sat around languidly nipping at the beer, me relating carefully selected bits and pieces of the last ten years while the night slipped away. I even told him a little about Beet.

"Beet? How'd he get a name like that?"

"His last name was Borak, and that's Polak for a beet farmer." I tried to bleed the emotion from my voice. "He was a great guy."

"Sounds like he was your bud. You know, your pal." He paused before adding. "Special."

"Yeah, he was. I mustered out and turned mercenary with him. That's how special he was."

"Guess guys get close like that when they're living and fighting together."

"It happens," I allowed. Had he sensed our true relationship?

"You ever kill anybody with your hands?" Another one from out of the blue.

"Yes," I answered quietly. This was getting a little intense.

"How did you do it? Cut the guy's throat?" I shook my head mutely. "Then how? Show me." He looked stricken. "Sorry, didn't mean to get so personal."

"If I show you, I might get carried away." I tried for some humor.

"That's okay," he responded. "I absolve you in advance."

"You might, but the law won't. Stand up," I ordered, my voice a little sharper than intended. As he rose, I slipped away from the fire and melted into the trees. A second later, I heard him call to me.

"Daniel? Where are you, man?"

I silently circled the camp. From his occasional shouts, I judged he was growing nervous. This wasn't the way he had planned for the game to go.

Understanding he would shift his stance continuously to watch for me, I eased behind a fat water oak directly to his left. When he turned to check another direction, I slipped up behind him and threw my left arm around his throat. My right thumb pressed gently against his carotid. He gave a strangled gasp and started to struggle, but quit when I pressed harder. His artery pulsed wildly beneath my thumb.

"That's the way I did it," I whispered with my lips against his ear. I eased the pressure but was loath to release him from my embrace.

He leaned against me in relief. "You scared the hell out of me, man. But...but it was sort of exciting, too. I didn't even hear you. I knew you were coming, but I never heard a thing."

"You weren't supposed to." My index finger flexed involuntarily against his cheek, caressing the light stubble of his invisible beard. His hair smelled clean and masculine. The length of his body rested against me, setting my groin afire. Abruptly, I released him and stepped away before any damage was done. "That's the way I did it," I said again.

"Awesome!" He rubbed his throat where my arm had been.

"No, it was horrible. It's an incredible high until you realize the thing lying at your feet had been a living, breathing man. Then the excitement leaches away fast."

"So you didn't like the killing part, huh?"

"No sane man likes it, Markey. And I certainly never did except—" I bit down on my tongue.

"Except when?"

"Except when I was killing the animals who slaughtered my...friend. And I wasn't too sane at the time." I drew a shaky breath. "Well, I'm turning in."

"Yeah, me, too. It's been a full day with my first buck and all. And...well, being with you. You know, hearing about your experiences."

"For me, too. It was good to see what kind of a man the kid next door grew up to be."

"A disappointment probably."

"Why would you say that? You're a handsome, healthy young man and a good person as far as I can see."

"Maybe. Sometimes I wonder."

"Anything you need to talk out?"

That slight hesitation and shake of the head again. "No. I'm okay."

Deciding to let him off the hook, I stripped to my skivvies and slipped into a sleeping bag laid out in the back of my SUV. Markey's white jockeys made his flesh seem even darker as he crawled into his own fart bag beside me. We said our good nights and a silence grew, broken only by the call of night creatures and the squawk of a loon somewhere at the far end of the lake.

"Daniel, is it true they drownproof you in BUD/S? How do they do that?"

"They tie your ass up and dump you in the water. The first thing you learn is not to panic. When you get over being afraid, you learn to bob your way to the surface and to the shore."

"Kinda like a real seal, huh?"

"Yep, just not as graceful."

He let the silence go on longer this time. "Daniel, I...I missed you, man. Thought about you a lot. Your mom used to let me read your letters."

"I missed you, too, kid."

"No you didn't. You were out there doing all kinds of exciting things. You didn't think about the pesky little kid back home."

"You'd be surprised. Mom kept me up on your life. I even have some pictures she sent."

"You do? Which pictures?"

"Photos of you in your football uniform, your graduation, things like that."

"Awesome. I thought you'd forgot all about me."

"No way, kid. You were my little brother, you know."

"And you were my..." The voice died away.

"Your what?"

"Idol, I guess."

I turned to face him. "That's not what you were going to say, is it?"

He dipped his head. "Daniel, if I tell you something, will you hate me?"

I chuckled softly. "I could never hate you, Markey."

"Don't be so sure. But never mind." He flopped over on his side.

I clasped his naked shoulder, pulling him onto his back. "Not so fast, buster. You can't give an intro like that and then just walk away from it. Say it, Markey, and trust me to handle it, okay?"

"I..." the voice dropped to a mumble. "I have feelings for you."

"So do I, buddy."

"No!" he cried in an anguished voice. "Not...not like that. I have *feelings* for you! I want to do things with you. But...but I don't know what!"

I swallowed hard. "What are you saying, kid?"

"Kid! Yeah, what are you saying, *kid*?"

"Sorry, but to an old dog like me, you are a kid."

A silence grew. *Well, you fucked that one,* I thought. I debated pushing him some more, and then he spoke.

"Daniel, how do you know if you're..."

"You're what?"

I sensed rather than saw his shrug. "Different."

"Everybody's different, Markey. That's what makes us who we are."

"I'm not talking psychology. I'm different."

I threw back my sleeping bag and came up to rest on my elbow. "Okay, man, it's time to talk turkey here. Say what you mean."

"How do you know if you're...well, gay?"

That one hit me between the eyes. "You try it with another man. If you want to slug him when it's over, then you're not. If you don't give a shit one way or the other, you were probably just experimenting. If you can't wait to try it again, then you probably are."

He turned to face me, and even in the faint light, I saw him examine my naked torso. "Who do you try it with?"

"Someone you like. A buddy. Someone who won't go berserk on you afterward."

His Adam's apple moved. "Can I try it with you?"

"Me?" My mouth went dry.

"Sorry," he backed off. "But I've been wanting to try it so bad. And I don't know anyone safe. I mean—"

"I know what you mean."

"I love you, Daniel," he said so softly I wasn't sure I heard him right.

"That's kind of fast, man. I just got back."

"No. I've loved you since before you went away," he said, swiveling his head away from me."

"You were only eight years old then."

"Didn't matter. I still felt that way. Thought maybe you felt it back. Nobody ever treated me like you did. Practically like a grown-up...like you were."

I laughed softly. "Shit, I wasn't even a grown-up myself."

"You were to me...the most grown-up guy I knew."

I put a palm to his cheek and turned his head to me. Silver shafts of light in the onyx corneas made them gleam like black fire.

"I didn't know," I whispered.

"Remember how I used to feel your muscles after we worked out? I always hoped you'd feel mine back, but you never did."

"Didn't mean I didn't want to."

"Did you?" he asked, flopping on his side to face me.

"Yeah, but I didn't have the nerve. If I had touched you, something would have happened, and you were too young. Hell, you probably didn't even know anything about things like that."

"Then how come I'd go home and play with my pecker afterward? The first time I came, Daniel, I was thinking of you."

I didn't know what to say, so I kept my mouth shut.

"I waited for you," he added. "I mean I haven't done it with anybody. Three guys wanted to get with me, but I turned them down."

"Three guys in Victor?" I asked incredulously. There couldn't have been three gays in that little burg, but, of course, it wouldn't just be gays trying to climb this guy's butt. Markey could make straights cream in their britches by just blinking those sable lashes...and he probably didn't even know it.

"Yeah, in Victor and, you know, on football trips. But I always said no because I was afraid it would make the picture I had of you...of us...go away."

"What about girls?"

"Well, I sort of did it to one."

I laughed aloud. "How do you sort of do it to a girl?"

His giggle was a release of nervous energy. "By trying it in the backseat of a car and not getting it in her very good. I came all over both of us."

"And you never went back to give it a proper try?"

His eyes glistened. "Too embarrassed. And besides, it wasn't like I thought it would be...like it would be with us. You know, you'n me."

"Kid, do you know what you're saying?"

"Making a fool out of myself, I guess. But, Daniel, I know what I want."

"And if you get it, it'll be like with that girl, a disappointment. You've got this romantic picture painted in your head, and that's not the way it will be. There'll be smells and emissions and sweat and grunting and—"

"Oh, man, I hope so! But that doesn't mean it won't be good, does it?"

That gave me pause. "Kid, it'll be earth-shaking for me, but I'm not sure how it will turn out for you. Nobody can know... not up front. And remember one thing. We could end up not being friends anymore."

He wrinkled his nose in the darkness. "How come? Why wouldn't we be friends? I mean, after something that awesome?"

"You might be so disgusted you won't want to lay eyes on me again."

"Maybe I don't *really* know how I'll feel afterward, but one thing I know for damned sure. I'll always want you for my friend, Daniel. You're a habit, man."

"Yeah, but maybe I'm a bad habit."

"No way." It got awfully quiet in the back of the SUV. Then he spoke again. "Course, you probably don't want *me* for a friend now you know I'm qu—uh, feel that way about you. But I finally got it out in the open, and it's been clogging up my insides for as long as I can remember. I just hope I don't pay too big a price for opening my big mouth."

He stirred restlessly as I grappled for an answer. I could have ignored my raging lust and eased him away gently, but he deserved honesty.

"No, Markey. You won't lose my friendship. If you don't know by now that I've got feelings for you, too, then I'm a better actor than I thought."

"You do?" he asked eagerly, those big eyes flashing ebony

light like an otherworldly alien. He reached for me but lost his
nerve; his hand fell into the space between us.

"Yeah, I do. How could I not? You're so fucking handsome...and sexy."

"I am?" The amazement was genuine. He had no idea how
hunky he was. "So...so what do we do now?"

"Markey, if you insist on this, then you're going for one hell
of a ride. When you come out the other side you'll either be
dazzled or revolted. Whichever way it is, I'm still available for
friendship. I just hope you are."

I rose to my elbow and leaned over him. His eyes were
huge, questioning, expectant. I lowered my lips to his, catching
him by surprise. He drew a sharp breath. After a moment, he
relaxed beneath my touch. Then he returned the kiss, his lips
softening, his mouth parting, his tongue timidly exploring. In
an explosion of breath, I ground my lips against his, glorying in
the electricity of the moment. When I drew away, he came with
me, holding on to my neck. He was halfway out of the sleeping
bag, his naked torso exciting even in the semidarkness. On his
knees, he rolled his jockeys down over his thighs. The shiny
glans of an engorged cock caught the moonlight, a glistening
pearl of precum at the slit.

Markey fell atop me, sending his thick erection down my
throat. His cry of pleasure conjured images of another cock,
a fat, throbbing column of living flesh I would never again
be privileged to take. With a sob, I threw him on his back
and examined him. He was larger than Beet...everything that
mattered was measured against Warren Borak...but not as
thick through the root. I tongued the slit and slipped my lips
over the bulbous crown, slowly riding the shaft to his groin,
burying my nose in his clean, black bush, drawing cries of
astonishment from his cherry lips. I slowly climbed the pole,

keeping up a slight suction as I reached the end. Then I tongued the underside down into his testicles. His legs spasmed before opening to my touch. I took the stones in my mouth, testing their firmness. Innocence, I thought. This was what innocence tasted like...firm, strong, clean, pulsing, exciting...fucking wonderful!

"Oh, Daniel!" he moaned as I moved a hand over his lean chest. "Oh, man! Oh, Danny! Oh...oh...oh..."

I came off him and licked my way to his chest with his excited cock throbbing against my chest. He shivered when I licked a nipple and groaned when I nipped the other. His breath came raggedly, his chest heaved. A fine sheen of sweat on his forehead shone in the gloomy truck.

"Do it again," he begged, his broad hands on my shoulders, pushing me back down his torso. I laughed softly as I tongued him all the way down into his curly bush. I held his bucking cock steady and went to work in earnest, washing the big glans and bobbing up and down on the shaft rhythmically. But it was another cock I took down my throat. A familiar shaft, a loving, comfortable column of flesh. I moaned his name in my head... *Beet! Beet! Beet!"*

"Ohhh, Daniel! I...I didn't know it would be...be so...so good!"

Finally, I began to discern differences. This column was longer, harder to take to the root. The aroma was different, the verbal entreaties not so gruff, the hands cradling my head more gentle. Beet slowly departed, bestowing a crooked smile on his successor.

Then, as his thinner, younger baritone vocalized his ecstasy, it was *Markey* I was pleasuring. I clasped his buttocks and pulled him up, lifting him off the floor of the vehicle. With a groan, he thrust his hips, driving his big cock into me, coming with a mighty roar and a geyser of tangy cum. The force of his contractions drove gouts of semen down my throat, almost strangling me. For a moment, I thought he had gone into convulsions. His body thrashed in my hands. He whined as he tried to force himself farther down my throat. Then he suddenly collapsed back onto the sleeping bag. Had he not been gasping desperately for oxygen, I would have feared he'd died of his efforts.

I held him in my mouth as that magnificent hard-on slowly softened. Giving the slit a final lick, I sat up beside him. His arm was across his eyes; my worst fears were realized. He was repulsed by shame and fear: shame at flaunting convention; fear of deviant longings.

Ignoring my own painful erection, I moved back to my own bag.

"Danny...uh, Daniel?" A hand caught my arm.

I paused. "Yeah, kid?"

"Can I try it? I mean, I won't do it good like you did, but can I try?"

"You want to suck me?" I asked, a smile lifting the corners of my mouth.

"Blow job. They call it a blow job, don't they?" He peeked out from beneath his arm.

I laughed aloud. "You bet they do! And don't worry about doing a good job. Touch me with those handsome lips, and I'll cum all over everything."

He pushed me on my back and hovered over me. Timidly, he tongued a nipple. I shivered in delight. After giving attention to the other one, he laid his head on my chest.

"You did this with him, didn't you?"

"Him? You mean Beet?" I considered lying, but this wasn't the time for it. "Yeah. How did you guess?"

"You said his name."

I laughed again. "I had a mouth full of cock at the time, how could you tell?"

He shrugged against my chest, sending goose bumps down my frame. "I just could."

I pulled him up to me. "Yeah, I did. I called to him. I had a ghost to lay away, Markey. And do you know what? He approves."

"He does? He approves me?"

"Absolutely, you handsome fucker."

"Can I try it now? I'll probably gag a lot, will that turn you off?"

"Gag all you want, my friend—"

"Lover," he interrupted me. "We went way beyond being friends tonight. I'm your lover now."

Amazed at the confidence in his young voice, I tousled his hair. "Lover. I like the sound of that."

"Mmm," he answered, slipping his lips over my leaking dick. He gagged, tried again and did better the second time. Then he came up and looked at me. "Did you do the other thing, too? You know, doing it to each other?"

"Yeah, we did," I answered, shoving his head down on me.

There was some more sucking and gagging. He came up again. "Are we going to do that, too?"

"You bet your good-looking ass!" I said. "But first you gotta finish this."

"Okay," he said with a grin and went back to work.

I've always had good orgasms, and those with Beet Borak were earth shaking. The first one with Marcus Markey didn't quite rise to that level, but it would only get better. Even as I exploded, and he valiantly struggled to take everything I could deliver, I fantasized about that *other thing* he was anxious to try.

DADDIES IN DAMIAN

Gavin Atlas

Through the kitchen window, Damian watched his boss, Stan, begin the job interview with the day's target. Damian had to lube up his ass in preparation for his cue. He usually felt nervous and aroused at this stage, but today there was also exhaustion. He'd been fucked constantly. Would there never be a break?

The target was as always, an older man, at least fifty, bearded. Damian loved being fucked and dominated by men more than twice his age, which made him perfect for Stan's project. This man looked attractive if overweight. He appeared a bit surprised to see Stan wearing a bathrobe for a job interview, but this was Hollywood, where business was often conducted poolside while sipping rum punches.

"Raymond, is it? Great to meet you," Stan said, shaking Raymond's hand without getting up or removing his sunglasses. "First, I need to let you know we tend to tape our interviews for our records, so please sign this release."

Raymond stroked his short beard and shrugged before signing. Damian knew the ad for the job was listed in the adult section, but it seemed that most men forgot that as they dressed up for the interview and brought résumés. Damian felt when the ad read, *International corporation seeks handsome, mature gay male,* they should know something related to sex was involved, but so many times the expressions of surprise were priceless.

"You'll oversee shipping of our products and monitor website traffic, among other duties," said Stan, gesturing from his lounge chair with one hand while holding a drink in the other. "First, I should confess that the pay is a bit lower than at other companies, but we do provide one perk to make up for it. Are you thirsty?" Stan hit the intercom button built into his lounger. "Damian, come here now," he ordered.

Nude, Damian opened the sliding glass door and headed straight for Raymond, drink in hand.

"Sweet mother of god." Raymond dropped the folder containing his resume and stared in wide-eyed amazement. "I apologize—I'm sure you didn't know I was here. I—"

"Not at all, Raymond," Stan said. "Damian is the perk I mentioned. I know it's not much, but we have to make do."

Raymond couldn't take his eyes off Damian. "He's gorgeous. He's an absolute Adonis."

Damian smiled but looked demurely away at Stan, focusing on the curls of white beard and salt-and-pepper hair. Stan had instructed Damian not to look at the target, so as to allow him to feast his eyes on Damian's body without temerity while Stan communicated Damian's willingness to fulfill a master's every need.

"Yes, yes, Damian's not bad to look at, but I'm afraid he's dumb as a post."

Damian's dick stiffened. He didn't want to enjoy the part

where Stan informed the target that he was just a stupid piece of ass, but he always did. He reminded himself that his English teacher back in Tennessee had told him he was bright enough for college.

"So it's a good thing you get to fuck his ass as part of the job," Stan continued. "Otherwise he'd be no use as an assistant."

Raymond nearly choked on his drink. "I beg your pardon?"

Stan shrugged apologetically. "I know this job can be a bit boring, and I'm afraid there are going to be times when you'll have nothing to do, so you'll be able to spend the whole day in Damian's ass if you wish. Why don't you try him out now to see if this is the right kind of workplace for you? Here, boy, get on all fours and offer yourself," Stan ordered, snapping his fingers.

A warm wave of humiliation washed over Damian, and now his weariness was eclipsed by the arousal he felt in his throat, his gut and his stiff dick. Why was he always so horny for debasement? He got into position to allow himself to be fucked doggie-style.

"Holy cow, that ass is amazing," Raymond murmured. "I can't believe—this has got to be some kind of joke you're playing on me."

Stan got up from his lounger, shaking his head. "Not a joke at all. Here, to prove it, I'll start fucking that hole first." Stan pulled out condoms from the pocket of his bathrobe and then slipped the bathrobe off. Stan was tall, perhaps six-three, and hairy. He'd tanned nude for years, and now his body had a leathery quality to it. Damian thought that Stan was too proud of his muscular physique, but Stan's extreme confidence and huge erection kept Damian in the mood to be submissive.

"This can't be happening," Raymond said as Stan sank his

dick into Damian. Even though Damian got fucked by Stan every day, there was always novelty when a new person watched them. The humiliation felt so good he was nearly delirious, but why couldn't his asshole ever be given a day off? He used to get them, but he hadn't had his ass to himself in more than a month.

As Damian began to grunt and moan, he wondered if Raymond was a "wise target." So many men had seen Stan's website that a number of the interviewees knew they were there to be videotaped fucking Damian.

"Take his mouth, Raymond," Stan said, his hands on his hips as he thrust in and out slowly. Damian could hear hurried unzipping and stripping. It wasn't another thirty seconds before Raymond pushed his cock between Damian's lips. He closed his eyes and concentrated on his breathing and the movement of his tongue over Raymond's cock, all the while keeping his ass arched to best accept his master's dick. He felt the tight pull of pleasure in his gut, but at the same time he thought to himself, *Damian, you have to stop this life sooner or later.*

Stan's thrusts increased in power and depth until with one final shove he climaxed with a growl, buried in Damian to the hilt. "God, this ass is good," Stan murmured and Damian closed his eyes in happiness at hearing he'd pleased his master.

"Your turn to take his rump," Stan told Raymond as he pulled out roughly. Either Raymond was wise to them or he'd become so rapt in his conquest of Damian's body that he could no longer find the words to express his disbelief in the direction the interview had taken. But as Raymond pushed his thick, sheathed dick into Damian's ass, he became vocal again.

"Damn, this ass feels incredible." Damian could feel Raymond's excitement and eagerness in the urgent thrusts and the vise-tight grip Raymond had on Damian's hips. Damian never tired of the older men who felt such ecstasy, such wondrous surprise at getting to fuck his hole. If only he could give such pleasure forever...

After being reamed for nearly ten minutes, Damian could sense Raymond closing in on his peak. With each thrust the older man pulled Damian's ass toward him to drive in ever deeper. Damian moaned with each punishing stroke until finally Raymond shot inside the condom, screaming with each wave of his orgasm. Then he collapsed on the bottom boy's back and whispered in his ear. "You're even better than I imagined."

As Raymond dressed, Stan made conversation about the interview process continuing, and how they'd certainly be in contact with Raymond in the near future. Damian remained obediently on all fours, suspecting that Stan knew Raymond was wise to the scene, but continued the interview anyway. What mattered most to Stan was that the target was an attractive Daddy type—and good at fucking.

After Raymond left, Stan's partner, Bob, emerged from his hiding spot in the den. "That taping was one of the best in the past couple months," he said as he kissed Stan on the cheek. Then he began to strip off his denim shorts. "And now my reward for all that hard work behind the camera is getting in your ass, Damian."

In response, Damian arched up his rear and waited for Bob's pounding penetration to begin.

Richard couldn't help but smile when he saw Damian bound up the stairs to his clinic. The young man's beauty and good nature never failed to delight him.

"Hey, handsome. Sit right down. Are you being careful?"

"Yes, sir, but I want to get checked anyway. Besides, it gives me a chance to see you."

"Big flirt," Richard said as he swabbed Damian's gums. The young men who came regularly to Richard's free STD clinic were almost all hustlers or participants in low-quality porn videos, the dangerous sort that demanded barebacking. Considering how often he had to distribute antibiotics or refer the boys to specialists, he was impressed that Damian was always negative for everything. He'd seen snippets of the website DaddiesinDamian.com and knew, from the videos, that scores of older men fucked the young stud.

"So this week when I have free time, I'm going to clean your gutters, cut your lawn and paint your side door."

"You already cleaned the gutters, Mr. Helpful, and you don't have to do anything, actually. This free clinic really is free."

"You can't be making much money treating people for nothing."

Richard shrugged. "So I don't have much money in the bank. The world won't end."

Damian gave Richard a simmering smile. "But I still want to help you because...well...I want you to like me."

"I do like you," Richard said, squeezing Damian's shoulder. "You're my buddy,"

"But you call all your patients 'buddy'. I want to be special."

Richard smiled but said nothing. Damian was special to the doctor, but Richard wanted to suppress the sentiment. Even though it had been two years, he was still wounded that Robbie, the only porn boy he'd ever allowed into his heart, had left him. But Damian was far more handsome and seemed so much sweeter. How could he not have feelings?

"You have such pretty eyes," Damian said. "They twinkle when you smile. And I like your beard and...you're so built for...um..."

Richard laughed. "For someone my age? I used to be a marine."

"Oh. That explains why you're so damn hot."

Richard couldn't help but grin. "Thank you, Damian." Richard knew he wasn't bad looking for an older man, but he was aware of how much Damian loved Daddies, so the compliment meant more than most, and a small wave of pleasure rippled through Richard's stomach.

"I don't have any money for a proper date, but can we maybe go for a walk in the park or something?"

Richard wanted to mention Robbie and explain why he didn't want to open up his heart, but took another tack.

"I do really like you, Damian, but I can't help but be jealous of all the men that fuck you. The right man for you to be with couldn't have that kind of hang up."

Damian frowned but nodded. "I understand. I've been meaning to get out of that situation. I figure I must have paid back Stan for the airfare from Tennessee, and I hope I'm earning more than what he expects for my room and board. He said he'd give me a chance to start college after the first year, and it's been almost three."

Richard knew that Damian had been in contact with Stan via the Internet and moved out to L.A. the day he turned eighteen. He'd had such a horrible relationship with his father and older brothers that he'd run away from home three times. Once he was eighteen, there was no way to drag him back. Damian had said he wouldn't have minded staying in the country and working on the family dairy farm, but not with the intolerance that surrounded him.

"Stan keeps wanting me to let guys bareback my ass for the website, but I won't."

Richard frowned. "If Stan promised college and isn't delivering, and if he is encouraging you to be unsafe, then yes, you should leave."

"Could I stay with you?"

Richard hesitated. There had been so many untrustworthy hustlers and unstable addicts coming through his clinic that he kept a Taser on hand. Damian seemed angelic compared to most of them, but he wasn't sure. "I...suppose, but maybe—"

"It's okay. I can tell you're uncomfortable with the idea. I'll figure something out."

That night Richard purchased a membership to DaddiesinDamian.com. The number of videos of Damian getting fucked numbered in the hundreds (the boy was only twenty!), and his dick stirred seeing how much Damian loved getting plowed by older men. On the other hand, it bothered him that many of the newest comments said things like, "If you want to keep me as a member, Damian needs to start getting barebacked." Others said, "Not just barebacked, but gangbanged."

With a little research, he was able to discover that the full name of the owner of DaddiesInDamian was Stan Latham. Digging deeper revealed that Latham had once been arrested for dealing crystal meth but got off on a technicality. Richard had figured Damian's "master" was up to no good, but this was worse than he expected. Maybe he would have to put past experience behind him and help Damian. Maybe he had to stop worrying about protecting his heart, at least for now.

Damian's depression briefly lifted when he saw the elation in Richard's eyes. Damian had brought a bouquet of daisies to Richard's house, and he wore his yard-work clothes, hoping to please Richard as much as possible.

"To what do I owe this pleasant surprise? Come in, young

man."

Damian looked down. "I have to leave Los Angeles, Dr. Preston. I made the mistake of getting on Stan's computer. I wanted to see how much money he was making from guys fucking my ass, and it's...a lot. I also saw some other stuff, and Stan and Bob caught me. Now they won't let me out of the house. I had to sneak out just to see you."

Damian saw the sadness in Richard's eyes. "Damian, don't go back. Call the police from here."

Damian shook his head. "I called the police before, and they won't do anything. Maybe Stan paid them off. Besides they have all my stuff, and I have nowhere else to go."

"Under the circumstances, it's completely fine to stay with me."

Damian smiled. "I would, but sooner or later Stan and Bob would find me and enslave my ass again. I don't want to get you involved in this mess. Over the past week, I was able to steal a dollar now and then to take the bus here and bring you flowers. I...uh...I also kind of...sold some gold cufflinks that belonged to Stan to a pawnshop, so I have enough for a ticket out of Los Angeles. I needed to say good-bye to you though."

"But you'll still need money for food and a place to stay."

Damian shuffled his feet. "I suppose I may have to let them fuck me for a while longer, and I admit part of me still enjoys it. Even if I'm starting to believe that I'm not good for anything except giving up my ass. It turns out I'm just as stupid as Stan says."

"Oh, sweetheart, you are not. One mistake made to get away from your family does not make you dumb."

Damian could no longer resist, and he leaned forward to kiss Richard fiercely, his lips pressed urgently against the older man's. He could sense Richard's surprise as he reflexively backed up, but then he returned the kiss, putting his arms around Damian and pulling him tighter.

"Please," Damian begged. "I may never see you again. Would you fuck me?"

Richard shut his eyes. He inhaled sharply, and then again, and a third time. Damian saw his resolve breaking.

"Yes! Yes, I want to fuck you so bad."

Damian felt himself lifted off the ground and gently carried into Richard's small house. Damian knew that with his muscular frame, he wasn't a lightweight, and Richard's strength surprised him. Every few steps, Richard stopped to kiss Damian's mouth, but in less than a minute, Richard had Damian on his back on the bed, kissing, nipping at and caressing the young man feverishly.

Damian couldn't control his need. He yanked off his shorts and put his legs in the air, moaning and squirming.

"Sweetheart, slow down. Let me be good to you."

"But sir, I'm so horny. Please, sir."

Richard continued his patient, affectionate exploration of Damian's body, caressing his muscular chest and abs, kissing his face and neck. Damian sighed in delight, but he still whimpered for penetration.

"Okay, okay. I want you just as bad as you want me," said Richard. He quickly stripped and Damian saw Richard's dick for the first time. It was hard and large. He was maybe a touch bigger than Stan, which meant Damian's hole would be stretched more than he was used to, but he'd be able to take what he was given with pure pleasure. Richard's taut body was even better than Damian had imagined, a vast improvement over most of the men who got to fuck his ass.

As Richard slipped on a condom, Damian pulled his knees back as far as he could to give complete access to his hole.

Richard let out a low rumble of appreciation as he lubed up Damian with two fingers and then three.

Damian was perplexed. He thought he loved the rough reamings he received from Stan, Bob and the men in the videos. But Richard's slow, gentle pace nearly sent him into a paroxysm of spent lust. He had to close his eyes and calm himself so as not to come too quickly. And suddenly, he was no longer in a hurry to leave Los Angeles before Stan found out he was missing. He wanted Richard's firm but loving penetration to last forever.

While Damian's pleasure at giving up his ass was intense, Richard's kisses were unfathomably wonderful. In the years with Stan, Damian had nearly never been kissed, and Richard's lips were so soft. His skin smelled clean and faintly of an aftershave Damian's father had worn. Damian inhaled deeply.

After Damian allowed Richard's tongue to find his, he felt Richard's cock stretch inside his ass. Damian whimpered in earnest from offering his hole so completely to such a huge dick, but instead of pushing Richard off, he surrendered, fully bringing his ankles to his ears. It was the most vulnerable his ass had ever been, and the euphoria filled Damian's chest to the point that he could barely breathe. Damian couldn't help it this time and with a great gasp, he came in huge spurts all over his neck and chin, his head thrashing left and right.

This set off Richard's orgasm, and with a series of grunts that turned to a roar, Richard climaxed, pushing his steel-hard rod as deep as possible on the last thrust. Damian was rewarded with the biggest, fiercest kiss he'd ever known. Then Richard looked down on him with an incredulous expression in his eyes.

"That was...so wonderful," Richard said. "I've seen clips of your videos, but I've never, ever seen you enjoy getting fucked so much."

"It's you," said Damian. "You're what made it better than all the other fuckings you've seen me take, and it's because you hold my heart."

Richard kissed Damian's lips. "You certainly know how to make a man feel happy, young fellow."

Damian felt a tendril of pleasure glide down his neck and spine as Richard ruffled his hair, but then there was a spike of sadness. "Now more than ever, I wish I didn't have to leave L.A."

Richard's face became serious. "I...I'm going to beg you to stay here, even if it's just for one night or a few hours. I want you to have a better plan than just taking a bus to anywhere. What if someone else gets you in the same situation?" Richard reached for his wallet. "Here, take forty dollars and buy some travel toiletries. Some extra underwear. I need to go close the clinic, but meet me back here in a couple hours. I plan to drive you at least a couple hundred miles out of L.A. to make sure you get away safe and sound."

Damian smiled with relief. "I would appreciate that so much, sir."

Damian did not return as promised. Richard worried, but he had no way to contact the young man. Over the next few days, he monitored DaddiesInDamian.com and was disappointed to see new videos appearing. Damian must have decided to stay. It upset him further that he could see Damian now had to argue over condoms each time. Stan appeared furious that Damian broke character as the perfect submissive, and Richard knew Damian would soon lose the safe sex battle.

On the fourth day after they'd made love, Damian called in tears.

"I was on my way back to your house, and they kidnapped

me off the street!" he said. "I called the police, but they couldn't care less about some fag porn boy, and now Stan says he's slipping me shit so I'll be arrested if I call the police again. I think it's true because I feel drugged and out of it."

Richard was horrified. "I'll think of something, baby. Just hang in there."

That night Richard studied the videos from Damian's site. The layout of the house wasn't evident; scenes were mostly shot by the pool. Richard noted that Stan and his cohort, Bob, were definitely big men. With his eyes always on Damian's body, he hadn't noticed they had the muscle necessary to keep a strapping farm boy prisoner. He felt the weight of his guilt in his chest. Why hadn't he trusted Damian before?

He set his mouth in determination. "Well," Richard said to himself, "they haven't tangled with a marine." He closed the porn site, opened a new document and began a résumé.

Damian could hardly believe his eyes. What was Dr. Preston doing here? He watched from the kitchen window awaiting his cue.

"Welcome, uh...Louis, is it?" Stan scanned Richard's fake C.V.

Richard nodded. "Quite a place you've got here."

"Why, thank you." Stan went through the same spiel he always did, making the job sound unappealing except for "one thing."

"In fact, why don't I show you what I mean," Stan said finally.

Damian heard the buzzer that let him know he was to bring out the rum punches. Richard was a good actor. He widened his eyes and looked stunned.

"You have a nude houseboy."

Stan smiled. "Do you like him? He's stupid, but he's a benefit."

Richard sipped his drink. "Benefit? In what way?"

"You get to fuck him as much as you want. He can't ever say no. It's all he's good for."

Damian trembled, worried he might give up the game.

"Well, let me see this fellow." Richard got up from his chair. As he approached Damian, he caught his toe on Stan's lounger and spilled rum punch on Stan's face and bathrobe.

"Oh, I'm so sorry. That robe looks like it costs a fortune. I hope it doesn't stain." Damian saw Richard drip something from what looked like an eyedrop bottle into Stan's punch. Damian immediately grabbed a towel and began drying Stan's head and face, hoping to keep Stan from seeing what Richard was doing. He also positioned himself so his backside blocked Bob's view.

"That's fucking enough, Damian!" Stan bellowed. "Get on all fours now!"

Damian complied.

"Why don't you enjoy Damian's ass?" Stan said.

Richard balked. "Right now? In front of you?"

"Of course. We're all very open here. I'll show you. I'll go first."

Stan, fully erect, slid off the soiled robe. Damian bent his head in shame, knowing Richard was about to see him humiliated.

"He's already lubed?" Richard asked as Stan slid inside Damian in one long stroke. "He lets you bareback his ass?"

Stan grunted. "Lubed, yes. He's lubed twenty-four/seven. Bareback. He doesn't have a choice."

Damian felt his face flush, wondering if Richard would still want him now.

"C'mon, get naked and get inside him, buddy." Stan waved

Richard over. "No need to be shy. You look like you have a great body under that suit." Stan stopped fucking to gulp his drink. Richard hadn't budged. "If you want the job, you need to start pumping his rump."

Richard nodded and stepped forward to stroke Damian's flank. "As soon as you're done, I'll fuck him like a madman."

"Fuck his ass now or get out of my house." Stan guzzled more rum punch.

Richard stripped off his shirt and had begun to unzip his pants when Damian felt Stan slow his thrusting. Stan mumbled something about his head and then slumped over, his dick popping out of Damian's ass.

Richard pulled Damian upright. "Quick, get some clothes!"

Damian shook his head. "Bob is watching! Look out, he's coming now!"

Bob was bigger and meaner than Stan, and Damian braced himself to witness him punching out Richard. But as the big man came at the doctor like a bull, Richard reached into his pocket, whipped around and struck Bob in the neck.

Bob went down instantly.

"What hap—"

"Taser. It won't keep him down long. Get clothes now."

"I don't have any. They got rid of them all!"

Richard raced to cover Damian with Stan's robe. "Do you have a wallet? Any kind of ID?"

"They locked it in their safe."

"Forget it. Let's go."

As they left Los Angeles on I-10, Damian kept letting Stan's robe fall open. Richard wouldn't have minded, but he reached over to cover the younger man. He didn't want trouble with the police.

"Where are we going?" Damian was still worried and periodically looked at the cars behind them. "What if Bob and Stan find out who you are and come after you?"

"We'll be fine. We'll put some distance between us and your captors, find a store and get you some clothes and then get out of the state."

"But where will we go? I thought you said you didn't have much money."

"I said I didn't have much money *in the bank*. I do have a lot of property, including a small ranch in New Mexico. Hey, there's a strip mall up ahead. What size shoes should I get? What size shirts and pants?"

Damian smiled and slid open his robe again. "For you, I wouldn't mind being nude all the time."

Richard smirked. "Yeah, but what if I want to take you to dinner? What if you want to take a college class?"

Damian's eyes widened. "You'd seriously help me with that?"

Richard's eyes glistened, and he interlaced the fingers of his right hand with Damian's. "I've wanted to help you for so long. I want to be your man."

Damian felt the warmth and affection radiating from Richard as they held hands. "I promise, from now on there's only going to be one Daddy in Damian."

Richard squeezed his hand. "That's right, handsome. And just you wait, this Daddy's gonna make everything all right."

SETTLING IN: LETTER TO JACK

Dominic Santi

Dear Jack,

There's been a lot going on here in the backwoods of Wisconsin. As you may have heard, this summer Eric and I finally moved into a new place—together.

I know, I know, after five years, it's about damn time. I admit that most of the holding out was my own doing. It's not just the age thing, though with me being twenty years older, sometimes I feel like his dad even when I'm not being his Dad, if you know what I mean. I swear, some days he's twenty-six going on thirteen. But we've worked out the age difference part pretty well.

Eric's just so damned irresponsible with his finances. He makes enough. In case you don't remember, he's got a college degree. He does computer programming for a company in town. He just doesn't know how to manage his money. Half the time he doesn't record his debits, though I paddle his butt every time an overdraft notice comes in. It really pisses me off. I've never bounced a check in my life. Personally, I think that's because when I was a kid, I got turned over my pop's knee whenever I screwed up. Eric had never been disciplined a day in his life until he met me.

The week after we moved out here, Eric's car died and he needed another one to get back and forth to work. His credit is so bad that the bank wouldn't finance him. Can't say as I blame them. When I finally agreed to cosign for the loan, I made it clear it was one thing for him to screw up his own credit, but he was not going to mess with mine. I was real blunt about it. I told him if he was so much as one day late on a payment, just one day, I'd take a switch to him. He agreed. I thought this time he'd manage to be responsible. After five years together, I suppose I should have known better.

Things went along pretty well for a couple of months. The new place is everything we've always wanted: out in the country, the upstairs half of an old farmhouse; no neighbors to speak of, except for the Pulaskis, a retired couple—our landlords—who live downstairs. We'll be watching the place for them in the winter while they're in Florida. Hell, there's even room for my vegetable garden. I have to admit, I've been feeling pretty damned domestic.

Then last Friday afternoon, Eric pulled into the driveway just as I was getting out of my car. Usually he gets home a half hour or so after me, so I figured something was up. He sounded real nonchalant when we walked in the door. That made me suspicious, especially after he hurried up the driveway ahead of me so he'd be the one getting the mail.

I pretended to be busy while he sorted through the day's delivery, mostly junk, but out of the corner of my eye I saw one of those yellow Insufficient Funds envelopes I'd learned to recognize from his earlier exploits. Eric paled and put the envelope in his pocket, but he didn't say anything, just went back to the bedroom to get out of his work clothes. I could feel myself starting to get hot. I knew his car payment had been due that week, but I decided to wait and see what he'd do. I'd changed and was reheating the spaghetti sauce for dinner when Eric finally came back into the kitchen. He leaned up against the counter next to me.

"Uh, Steve?" He was looking really nervous and tried to cover it by fiddling with the salt shaker. "Um, I had a little problem with the bank today. Nothing serious," he said quickly, like he was trying to reassure me. "I took care of it already. But I figured I'd better tell you. You're busy. We can talk about it later."

Eric was nodding a lot as he talked. As he finished he turned like he was going to walk back into the other room. He froze in midstep when I turned the sauce off and said, "I'm not busy at all. What's up?"

I think he recognized the chill in my voice. I was trying to keep my temper under control, even though I was relieved he was being man enough to admit having screwed up. Honesty is important to me, especially now that we have a home life together. But damn, I was mad at that boy. The week before he'd bought another fancy new video game. I was willing to bet money he hadn't recorded the transaction, at least until it was too late.

Eric hemmed and hawed around the topic, but he finally confessed to writing a bad check for the car payment because—you guessed it—he hadn't recorded the other debit and a couple more besides. He'd suddenly remembered that morning, but by then it was too late.

"I transferred the money from savings though," he said, still nodding vigorously. "The bank said the payment is credited as of today, so it's all taken care of. There's nothing for you to worry about."

"But my credit record still shows a late payment on a loan I cosigned for," I said coldly.

"Well, yeah," he blushed. "But like I said, I took care of it."

"Then there's something else we need to take care of," I said sternly. "What did I tell you would happen if you were late?"

"Now Steve, th-there's no cause to be hasty," he stammered. His eyes were big as an owl's. I could tell he was nervous, but I wasn't in the mood to put up with any of his guff. Times like this, I really wish his father had done his job.

"I'm not being hasty, boy," I said. "I'm angry. And you're going to get what's coming to you. Go downstairs and get a switch from the poplar tree."

"Dammit, Steve! It's just a car payment!" he fumed.

"Yes, it is." I said coldly. "One that you purchased using my credit, and now I've got a late payment on my record. I warned you, Eric. I told you what I'd do if this happened, but you didn't pay one lick of attention. Now you go downstairs and get a switch, or so help me, boy, if I have get it myself, I'll break it over your butt!"

He argued a bit more, a one-sided conversation that I didn't bother to join in. When I'd finally had enough and started for the door, Eric stormed past me and stomped off down the stairs, muttering under his breath. But he went. You see, it isn't just a matter of getting a switch. The poplar tree belongs to our land-lords. He had to ask permission to cut it.

I stood out on the balcony and listened to him knocking at their door. Old man Pulaski answered. He's almost deaf so you really have to yell when you're talking to him, and most of the time he doesn't bother to wear his hearing aid. That's one of the things we really liked about the house: lots of privacy.

Eric was trying to be quiet, mumbling about wanting to cut a branch from the tree. Finally, I got tired of Mr. P's "huhs?"

and "whats?" as Eric danced around the topic. I leaned over the balcony and hollered, "Eric wants to cut a switch from your poplar tree because he needs to get his ass whipped."

Eric looked up and gave me a really evil look as Mr. Pulaski laughed and said, "That true, boy?"

"Yes, sir," Eric muttered, turning every shade of red you can imagine as he kicked a rock off the sidewalk.

"What did you do?" Mr. Pulaski asked, stepping out onto the porch.

"I was late with my car payment," Eric shrugged. "Nothing serious."

Suddenly a cane swung out and whapped Eric on the thigh. "It sure as hell is serious, boy! You young fellas need to learn to be responsible."

"Ouch!" Eric yelped, jumping back and rubbing his thigh. He frowned up at me even harder, like it was my fault he'd gotten hit.

"You really gonna whup him, Steve?" Mr. Pulaski hollered up at me as he hobbled out into the yard, leaning on his cane.

"I sure am," I said, nodding in the affirmative.

He nodded his approval. "Good for you. That poplar tree helped me raise five boys and they all turned out just fine. I think a whipping is just what this young pup needs."

Mr. Pulaski turned around and swatted Eric again with his cane. "You come with me. I'll help you pick out a good switch, boy, one that'll get the job done proper so you're not out here cutting another one next week."

If I hadn't still been so mad, I would have burst out laughing at the look on Eric's face. Mr. Pulaski took out his pocketknife and hobbled over to the tree, telling Eric exactly which branch to cut and where. Eric sure didn't look very happy. He cut a long, sturdy switch, probably a good deal thicker than he would have chosen on his own and full of twiggy branches. When Mr. Pulaski took it from him and swung it once against Eric's thigh to test it, Eric yelped and jumped back a good three feet. The look of surprise on his face let me know that he was just figuring out how much that switch was going to sting.

Mr. Pulaski shoved the switch back into Eric's hands and turned him toward the steps, giving him a running commentary on how lucky he was to have someone who cared enough about him to whip him when he needed it. The look on Eric's face told me he didn't share the old man's opinion. He was muttering under his breath again as he started up the stairs.

Mr. Pulaski was almost to his own porch when he looked up at me and said, "Steve, since I'm letting you use one of my switches, you be sure you do it right. A whuppin' over clothes never did anybody a lick of good. You make him take down his pants and you whip his ass bare. You hear me?" He pointed his cane up at me. "I'm gonna put my hearing aid in and I expect to be able to hear that switch doing its job. If that boy ain't yelling his head off, you're not doing it right!"

"Yes, sir, Mr. Pulaski," I said, looking Eric right in the eye. "I'll do just that."

"Now wait a minute, Steve," Eric protested as he finished climbing the stairs. I jerked my head at him and he reluctantly walked in the door. "You're not really going to do what he said, are you?" He was shaking his head, trying to laugh it off. "Damn. He really is a crazy old coot."

"No, Eric. I'm not going to make you take your pants down," I snapped. He stopped dead in his tracks at the tone of my voice. I think he was finally realizing just how pissed off I was. "I'm going to make you take your pants off. In fact, you're going to take everything off. Do it, *now*!"

As I spoke, I jerked one of the kitchen chairs over into the living room, right into the open space by the screen door where the sound would carry out and down the stairs.

"Now wait a minute!" Eric was trying to sound angry though he sounded more scared than anything. His hands were shaking as I yanked the switch from them.

For a moment we stood, staring each other down. Then I said very quietly, "After all the money problems you've had, you know I had real reservations about giving you another chance, especially one that affected my credit history. But as part of my commitment to our home life, I agreed to cosign that loan for you. You agreed to make the payments on time and to take the consequences if you made a payment late. Are you going back on your word to me now?"

Eric looked at me, shifting from foot to foot like he was trying to find some sort of magic answer to pull out of the air. We both knew there was a lot at stake between us. Finally he blew out a long breath and looked away, shaking his head. "No, sir. I'm not going back on my word. I screwed up. I'll take the whipping."

He looked back at me and smiled weakly. "I'm just a little nervous, okay? I mean, I've never been whipped before, and that thing looks like it'll really sting!" As he spoke, he unconsciously rubbed the spot on his thigh where Mr. Pulaski had swatted him.

I have to admit, I was relieved. Eric really is a good kid, in spite of how mad he makes me sometimes. I settled down to business.

"Eric," I said as I took him firmly by the shoulder and steered him to the chair, "this switch isn't just going to sting. It's going to burn pure fire over every inch of your bare butt!" He looked up at me, startled. His eyes got even bigger as I stepped back and motioned for him to get ready. "By the time I'm done with you, you're going to be yelling so loudly Mr. Pulaski will probably be able to hear you without his hearing aid, and you'll be ready to beg that bank to take your payments early so that you never have to go through this again. Now strip! And I mean everything off but your socks, boy! Move it!"

Eric's hands were shaking and he was as pale as I've ever seen him, but he nodded and started unbuttoning his fly. As I watched, he shoved his jeans down over his hips, kicked off his shoes and worked his jeans over his feet. A minute later, his crisp white jockeys and his T-shirt were also folded in a neat pile on the kitchen table. He stood shivering as I finished peeling the excess leaves off the switch.

"Bend over the back of the chair and grab the lower rung, the one beneath the seat," I said firmly.

He looked really nervous, but I have to give him credit. Scared as he was, Eric followed my directions, and a minute later, he was in position, his butt in the air and his privates pulled up out of the way so I had a clear shot at his ass.

I did take a minute to admire the view. Eric has a gorgeous ass, full and cream-colored and naturally as smooth as a baby's behind. But I was determined not to let my interest in his assets distract me. Eric was depending on me to give him the discipline he needed. I was determined to paint his pretty little butt with that switch until he'd learned his lesson.

He suddenly lifted his head up and looked back over his shoulder at me, licking his lips as he stammered out, "Uh, Steve? How m-many are you going to give me?"

I wasn't going to play that game. "As many as you need," I said firmly, stepping into position in back of him. "That'll sure as hell be long after Mr. Pulaski gets tired of hearing you howling."

With that, I drew back my arm and swung. The branch hissed through the air, landing against that creamy skin with the distinctive *swish crack!* of a really good switch. I felt the vibration travel up my arm at the contact.

Eric gasped. A second later, a red line appeared on that pale skin and the secondary burn settled in. He let out a startled, "*Yeowch!*" and straightened up fast, grabbing his butt with both hands.

He turned around and looked at me with huge, scared eyes. "Shit, Steve, that really hurt!"

I nodded my agreement. "You're damn right it did. And it's going to hurt a whole lot more before I'm done. Get back into position, unless you need me to tie you down."

Eric stood there for the longest time, just looking at me. Then he took a deep shaky breath and said, "No, sir. You don't need to tie me. I'll h-hold still."

With that, he took another deep breath, tucked up his privates again, and bent back over the chair. I was really proud of that boy. This time, he knew what was coming, and he was still man enough to take his punishment.

When Eric was back in position, I said, "Are you ready?"

"Yes, sir," he whispered shakily.

I drew back my arm, and I commenced to whipping that boy's ass with that switch.

Swish crack!

"Ow! *Ow! OW!*"

I waited between strokes, letting the first sharp burn then the blaze of the after sting sear into his butt, so that he felt the full effect of each one.

"Oh, please, Steve, please no more!" he cried out after the fourth stroke , twisting against the chair as he stiffened up onto his toes, but he didn't try to get up again. "Damn, that hurts!"

"I haven't even started yet," I snapped, "and it's supposed to hurt!"

Swish crack!!! He yowled again.

I could hear the tears starting in his voice. But I was determined to make enough of an impression on him that I wouldn't have to whip him like that ever again.

"You will be responsible!" I snapped. "Do you hear me, Eric?" *Swish crack!* "You will make your car payments on time," *Swish crack!!* "And you will be responsible with your finances!" *Swish crack!!!*

Each stroke raised a long, dark welt, the edges deeply defined and surrounded by a spiderweb of thin pink lines from the outer twigs. Eric howled with each stroke, his entire butt quickly flushing bright red as I blistered him from the top of his firm young ass to the tender skin where his thighs met his lower cheeks.

Eric was hollering at the top of his lungs by then, pleading he'd had enough and promising he'd never do it again. He was being so loud I'd be surprised if Mr. Pulaski didn't have to turn his hearing aid off. I knew how much that switch burned. Like I said, my pop made sure I got it when I needed it. But I still whipped that boy's butt at least a dozen times more. By the time I was done, every inch of Eric's backside glowed beet-red and looked like it was laced with bee stings. Eric was bawling his eyes out. But he really needed that whipping, and I damn well gave it to him.

Eric didn't even try to put his clothes on the rest of that night. He walked around naked, snuffling every once in a while and needing lots of hugs and reassurances of my affection. And when he went to bed right after dinner, I jerked him off while I rubbed some cream into his sore, hot butt and told him the matter was over, so he understood the discipline is part of how much I love him.

The next day, Eric apologized again, this time sincerely, for the late payment. He sealed the deal with a blow job that damn near knocked me flat. Monday morning, he set up an automatic payroll deduction to take care of his car payment, though he said he plans to check it each month, just in case. Not the way I do things, but he finally appears to be learning to manage his finances in a way that works for him.

Mr. Pulaski, well, he's given us his permanent permission to cut as many switches as we need for me to keep my boy in line. Eric even thanked him, though he stood back out of the way of that cane when he did it. But they were both smiling. Like I said, Eric's a good kid, he just needs his Dad to make sure he doesn't step out of line.

I'll write again soon. Hope things are going well in your neck of the woods.

Steve

NEVER SAY
NEVER AGAIN

Dale Chase

He is breaking every rule and it's giving me a hard-on. Sitting at my office desk, I think to lock the door because if I keep on reading his story I'm going to have to address my need, and I am going to keep on reading because it's the best work I've seen in some time. I teach the rules of fiction and students often break those rules and make a mess, but once in a blue moon a kid not only breaks the rules, he throws them out entirely, like he hasn't listened to me at all but only to himself, following an instinct that overpowers anything anybody will ever tell him. That's Harley Keith, the eighteen-year-old freshman whose work is at hand.

I do lock the door. My next student appointment isn't for half an hour and at the rate I'm going, I'll only need a couple of minutes. I haven't done this in ages. I've kept the proper student-teacher distance for three years, keeping on keeping on, as they say. My cock remains in my pants and I address personal needs in the privacy of my home, but now I've been ambushed. It's his first paper. The school year has just begun.

Sitting back in my chair, I unzip, get a hand on myself, then realize I'll need a come rag and the thought both amuses and disgusts me. I'm fifty-two, a tenured and well-respected academic. I shouldn't be abusing my dick but it's blissfully hard and I'm not going to let it go. In the bottom drawer I find what I'm looking for, the old rag, stiff with three-year-old issue from back when I fell for Cody Morse, also a freshman but let's not go there. I take up the rag, place it nearby, then pick up Harley's story in my left hand, get my dick in my right. And I am home.

His sentences run together and his commas are a disaster but his word selection is wrenching in the best way. He writes from a father's viewpoint about a mother and son who share such a powerful love that the father is excluded. That an eighteen-year-old can capture the father's concealed anguish amazes me and even though I'm reading the father, I'm feeling the writer so I'm jerking off to a family scene, which makes no sense because in itself it's not arousing. But Harley is there, onstage and brilliant, writing with such fury that I pump my cock and before I can finish the story I am spurting come in a glorious and surprising release. I work myself until the climax subsides and even then tug and squeeze because I want this boy.

Cleaning up, I am disgusted, and once the come rag is back in its drawer to further stiffen, I take red pencil to Harley's story, marking his errors, reminding him of rules. Once I'm done I realize I've gone too far because it is, after all, brilliant. Reading it aroused me so some credit must be due. I make a margin note that sometimes rules should be broken and that he has a good style that needs to be reined in a bit. Grade: B.

He sits in the second row and doesn't slouch like most. He also doesn't come to class wired to earbuds and whatever the others carry in shirt pockets. His posture is erect. There's no other way to describe that back. And he fixes on me and doesn't take notes, as if he can absorb what I'm saying so he can discard it.

He is not especially handsome. His brown hair is straight and longer than the others who favor buzz cuts, spikes, and baseball hats worn backward. He is fair skinned and possibly a dweeb by student standards. I cannot tell on this point as he is quite animal to me, crouched and ready to pounce but selective about his prey. And students do prey on old men.

As if sensing my interest, he stops me after class next day to make an appointment to see me. Office hours are from two to four on Tuesdays and Thursdays. I tell him he can have three o'clock on Thursday and he nods, offers a quiet thank-you. He is well mannered, low keyed, yet carries a sexual aura that all but roars.

At home where I have lived alone since Carl died, I attempt my usual order but know it futile. From the moment I step inside I want to come and I want to do it while thinking of Harley Keith. But I look through the mail, turn on the TV to catch the news, change into sweats, put dinner into the microwave. I manage to keep order until around eight when I turn off the TV, get naked, get out Harley's story—the only one I've brought home—and settle onto the sofa with lube and a towel.

He will be relatively hairless, I decide, smooth and pink with a small patch of brown between his legs. His prick will be hard much of the time and I picture him with his hand on it now, stroking in time to my effort. I read his story again, coming partway through, pages scattered to the floor as I shoot a surprisingly good load up my front. And after this I lie spent, picturing the boy hard again because eighteen-year-olds are relentless and I see myself kneeling before him, sucking his cock that tastes of his earlier come. I can almost feel him buck and my tongue involuntarily laps at the absent jizz.

* * *

Next day my step is lighter as I attempt to keep down the budding crush or whatever in hell Harley Keith has set upon me. I teach two other classes because it is Tuesday and Harley's class is Monday, Wednesday and Friday. So I am free of him yet find myself wondering who else he is terrorizing. Does he have Wayland for English Lit? Wayland who fucks everything that moves? Or maybe Jackson, the math guy who's married but jerks off in the teachers' bathroom? If I start adding it up, more of the faculty is after boys than girls. I am one of many, even as I feel so apart. What I have for Harley is born of his talent for words, his genius.

By the time Thursday office hours arrive, I'm a happy wreck. My cock hasn't had such a workout since I don't know when and there's a fresh come rag in my office drawer. I jerk off in the shower morning and night. I could barely get it up after Carl died. It was Cody Morse who got my juices flowing again but with disastrous results. And since then there has been a determination to never again so indulge. But now I awaken hard every morning. My cock stirs at the sight of young men and when I see Harley, it fills and aims, begging me to follow. So when I am behind my desk at the appointed hour, I am already hard. And then the boy comes into the room, flushed, hair tousled, ten minutes late.

"Sorry, professor," he says. "I got caught up in a discussion with a couple of jerks and you know how that is."

I nod, amused by his easy familiarity. He settles into the chair opposite but not before I get a look at his crotch where I find what I want, the roundness of a half-hard dick.

He is dressed in jeans and a light-blue polo shirt, appearing grown up even as his face looks younger than the rest. His voice is soft, hesitant, an easy baritone. *Does he sing? Would he sing for me?*

"Now what can I help you with?" I ask.

"It's about my story," he says as he pulls it from his backpack. He leans forward, radiating an intensity that builds like a cock rising. "Your comments and all the red. I don't understand. I mean, I understand there are rules of composition, but this isn't some essay, it's life and you said that's what you wanted. It's real."

"And then some," I offer which seems to puzzle him.

I would like to get up, go around the desk and perch upon the edge as professors do in the movies but we'd have to address my prick and that's not a good idea just yet so I stay put, attempt to remain academic. "Reality is not the basis of fiction, I don't care what television says. Listen to yourself, make something up and try to stay within the rules of composition, however constraining they might feel. Your story is powerful, you portray vivid scenes and your characters are well drawn, but there's an underlying chaos that would make an editor toss it. Sometimes you have to compromise. You can turn yourself loose on the page to some degree but not entirely."

Oh, how I want to pull out my dick, for this is beyond exciting. It would take just a stroke or two to get off. Or he could suck the thing. I clear my throat as the image sets my heart racing. "I hope you understand," I rasp. I reach for my water bottle, take a swig. "Please don't take the criticism personally as it's not intended that way. I am offering guidance. And I very much look forward to your next story."

"I'm working on it, but what you said about this one sort of upset things."

"A writer must develop not only his talent but a thick skin. Criticism will always be part of the writer's life. You must learn to listen, weigh, sort and choose to embrace it or not. You have talent, Harley. Now work with it, get it into shape, reel it in a bit and you'll find it works all the better."

He relaxes with my assurance. He settles into the chair, puts his story into the backpack, smiles. Now would be the time to fuck him. He'd be receptive, grateful, but I keep this to myself. When he rises I do not. "I'm available any time you have questions or concerns," I tell him and he replies with thanks. And then he is gone.

Leaping up, I lock the door, get out the fresh come rag, and settle back to free my cock. Before I take hold, I replay everything about our encounter, listening to him again, seeing him sit forward as he expresses his unrest. I see the bulge of cock and with this image I grab my own, stroking as he might until I erupt. It is prodigious, as befits my feelings. A promising boy does stir the pot.

When I finally fuck Harley Keith it is in my office. We are six weeks into the semester and the boy is harnessing his creativity, giving me powerful stories that hit me in heart, gut and crotch. I try not to jerk off while reading them because they deserve better, but I still do jerk off. And then one day during office hours Harley bursts in without an appointment, apologizing as he slams the door behind him. "I don't get it," he says, flinging pages at me. "You tell me to write what I feel, but you still tear it apart. What the fuck do you want?"

He is red faced, breathing hard and so pent up I know he needs to fuck. Maybe that's the problem. Maybe he can't handle criticism when he hasn't gotten off. His uttering the word *fuck,* in any context, confirms the need.

"Harley," I soothe, "Harley." I get up, come around the desk, and he lets me take him by the shoulders. "I am sorry if I upset you. That is not my intent. Never do I wish to cause you pain of any kind, but I must be honest about your work and this latest is a return to your early chaos. You'd been making such progress, producing fine work, then you give me this borderline nonsense. Even your style is lost amid the ravings."

He slumps beneath my touch, but I hold on. "Tell me, is something going on in your life that has upset you?" I ask. "The work seems to say that."

He shakes his head in the negative but starts to speak. "This guy: we broke up, I wasn't expecting it and we had this scene and everybody saw it which made it worse and there were names called and oh, god, I'm a wreck. I mean, I really cared for him and he just shit on me."

"I am so sorry," I say, folding him into my arms. The gesture is without intent, merely the comforting of a boy in pain, but my dick isn't buying that.

Harley doesn't resist my consolation and I pass a grateful second that I have some appeal. I slide my arms down his back, pulling him close and his arms wrap around my neck. A shudder runs through him and I think there may be tears. I am moved to offer homilies. "It will be all right, it will be all right."

Seconds pass in this comforting state, and as I feel him resurrect his upright posture, he starts pressing his crotch to mine. I am tentative in my response, allowing just slight pressure, but he is suddenly rampant, humping me until I tell him he must lock the door. When he pulls away I see him wild eyed, flushed. He's panting and he rushes to seal us in, then drops his pants and stands before me. His cock is ample, cut, and bright pink and for a second I recall my dreams of kneeling before him.

"You must let me fuck you," I say as I kneel, "but first I must feed."

He comes almost the second I get my mouth onto him. I need do little more than receive his offering, sucking and swallowing as he thrusts and spurts. He grunts and moans softly and I take these in as eagerly as I do his spunk and then he is done, the morsel softens, but I still suck for it has been some time since I've been so engaged. Finally I withdraw because my own cock begs attention.

"Take off your pants," I tell him as I clear a spot on the desk, find a condom. He responds while I push down my own pants and underwear, freeing myself. "Get onto the desk," I tell him, "on your back."

He gets into position and before I can instruct him further, pulls his legs high and wide. And there it is, the dark center I crave. I apply the rubber, wet myself with spit, and look at his face before I go in. His mouth is open, tongue out just enough to offer welcome.

I ease into him and for a second I simply idle, home at last. His passage is tight, befitting his age, and he wriggles a bit as if to get me going. I smile, start to thrust and he grabs his cock, holds on.

It is a gloriously good fuck, one of the best of my life and at fifty-two there have been quite a number. But there is nothing like giving it to a beautiful boy, a genius boy, a boy full of promise who has much to offer the world, a boy who sets all aside to raise his legs for me.

I take my time. The best part of age is loss of the damnable urgency that cuts you short all too often. I know how to drive my dick, how to ease up to make things last, how to savor the feel of the push and pull. I am inside this boy. I have him. I allow my dick to pop out and I drive it up between his legs so I can see it hard, fucking hard, then I ram it back in because minutes are ticking by and I can't do this all day, much as I'd like to. And the stir is beckoning and what man can resist that particular rise. So I pick up speed until I'm shooting into him, unleashing what feels like every ounce of fluid I possess in every organ I possess. And Harley is working his cock and starts to spurt and my ecstasy is doubled with us both letting to at once, awash in come young and old.

Finally I must relent because I am empty. I slide out, toss the condom, and pull Harley to his feet. He allows me to kiss him. His lips are soft and willing and were we not in my office, I would get him going again but we must stop. I retreat, tell him it was wonderful, and we dress. As he picks up his backpack and prepares to leave, I make an offering.

"I am available to you night and day," I say. "For any reason."

He studies me, still sheepish, as if we've done no more than discuss his work. He nods and then he is gone.

When a student comes in twenty minutes later for a scheduled appointment, it is a trial to pay attention but I manage. And when she is gone, I hurry to wrap up and get out of the building because I want to get home, fix a drink and replay Harley's every detail. So I'm full steam down the hall when a rushing student crashes into me. And it is none other than Cody Morse.

I teach my students that circumstance must never be used in their work even when it does, in fact, pervade real life. We encounter improbability all the time. A man travels to India and finds his dentist at the same hotel. A woman moves to another state and her next-door neighbor is the cousin of her sister-in-law. It's there all the time but must never appear in fiction, lest the reader see it as an easy out and feel cheated. Cody Morse on this day is pure circumstance, but it doesn't lessen the impact. The incident is brief, we pass a look, and I hurry away. He does the same but I'd venture with less fallout.

In my car I begin to swear. My hands are shaking so badly

I drop my keys and I leave them on the floor as I sit uttering all manner of epithets, none of which relieve the pain of his intrusion. "Fuck, shit, goddamn fucking shit," and on and on until I run out and sit like some dazed victim.

Carl and I were together twenty-six years. Carl Perry, master plumber and twenty years my senior; Carl, the man who took up the raw student and taught him about sex and life. Plumbers can be more than the grunting man snaking out the toilet. They can be surprisingly well read, witty, sexy and above all caring. That was Carl. He supported me as I pursued my degrees, encouraged me with the teaching job, and stuck by when I had to overcome sexual discrimination to gain tenure. He was my life and when his heart failed and he departed at sixty-eight, I was bereft. My lover, my mentor, had gone. The emptiness was of such enormity that I nearly lost my job and at times considered packing in my life. There would never be another Carl because, without him, I slipped into his older-man realm, which I'd never considered myself part of until I found myself alone.

How is a man to make such a transition? I had adored his embrace. A bear of a man, he babied me terribly. He petted and consoled, he loved and fucked. He taught me life's perspective, which is possibly the best lesson of all. And then he left me to take up his role. It seemed impossible.

He died in July, so I had six weeks until the fall semester. On the first day of classes I was annoyed by the crush of students and was shaky in front of my class. I began Fiction Writing by parroting myself because I could not summon the energy to create anything new, and it worked fine and I got things going; I began to surface. And then Cody Morse arrived, a latecomer who eyed me with such certainty that I knew he had been sent to ease my burden.

He had a farm boy quality, rough and unkempt. He always

wore rumpled khakis, never jeans, and a battered brown leather jacket over dingy T-shirts.

He approached me after class his first day, said he wanted to be a writer, wanted to know who to read. I told him all would be covered in class but he fidgeted with such impatience that I crossed a line I'd never before considered. "I could tutor you privately if you like," I offered.

He grinned. "That would be great. When can we start?"

I knew what was going to happen and so did he because he adjusted his cock as he spoke. We set a time for him to come by the house one evening. "Give it a try," I said.

"Cool."

I fucked him the first night and every tutoring session thereafter. Oh, we did the tutoring but always in languid discussion after sex, me petting and playing while he went on about his ambitions. He had genuine creative talent and I did encourage him to the fullest, but there was always desire involved. I needed him and within this saw how Carl had needed me, and I took a measure of satisfaction in assuming that role, as if Carl were inside me now, cheering me on or at least nodding with approval. I was guiding a boy into his destiny while the boy freed me from grief.

It lasted three and one half months. Cody ultimately spent more than tutoring sessions at my house and we started having daylong sexual wallows that were a true awakening. As my house is well fenced, we ran naked outside until the weather drove us indoors where we coupled before a roaring fire.

During this time Cody blossomed as a writer, displaying remarkable originality along with strong command of language. His father was a railroad man who liked to read, so Cody had grown up at the library and been encouraged in words and thinking, but his father had also rejected the gay boy, so there was anger grown alongside the talent. Cody was one of the few young men I encountered who was able to channel one into the other by way of writing. That he didn't write about fathers and sons mattered little. His anger was on the page, not specific but fuel nevertheless. It spilled out like flaming gasoline and I couldn't get enough.

And then one day when I expected him at the house, he didn't arrive and I phoned but got only his machine.

At first I left playful inquires as to his whereabouts, saying I was ready and waiting, but these soon deteriorated into demands. *We had plans, he was expected.* For two days he was a no-show and then there he was in class and I was tipped over and unable to right myself, struggling through the hour. For the first time Cody asked no questions, offered no comments. He sat slouched in his chair, taking no notes, looking like he'd been roughed up more than usual.

He knew what he was doing to me. He knew I loved him and he sat there and allowed me to stew in those awful juices. "Mr. Morse, may I see you?" I called out as any professor might at the end of class. He dropped back down into his chair and let the room empty.

Neither of us spoke at first. I hoped he might initiate some apology but when none came I went to him and asked in as light a voice as I could manage, "What's going on?"

"What do you mean?" he said, like he hadn't a clue that anything had shifted or more, that he'd done the shifting.

"I expected you Sunday. We had plans."

"Oh, yeah, right. Something came up."

"And tutoring on Monday?"

"Something else came up." He didn't grin but he might as well have, and I felt a hot stab to my middle because I knew what he meant. He'd had another man's dick, one preferable to mine.

"Are you telling me..." I couldn't finish the question because I feared the answer.

He stood up. "I don't think I need any more tutoring. Got the hang of it now."

I shut my eyes because I was dying inside and so was the Carl that had come alive in me. It was all imploding and I had to sit there and take it, allow shrapnel to tear my guts to pieces, all because this little shit had found somebody better. And probably younger. "I suppose you do," I managed, and he shrugged and was gone.

Roger Bruxton found me sitting, slumped, when he came in to start his French Literature class. "Merrill? Are you all right?"

"Yes, of course." I stood but my knees nearly buckled and Roger, fifteen years my junior, rushed over. "I'm fine," I insisted somewhat harshly, then apologized and he dismissed my attitude with the good humor of a young man indulging an older one. I gathered my papers and briefcase with some effort and hurried from the room, rushing to my car where I burst into tears.

Now I suffer the worst kind of déjà vu, abandonment rising up to consume what has just begun to sprout. People are passing by the car and when one looks in I start the engine and drive away, wiping tears so I can see the road. I don't go home, though. I drive to the beach where I don't get out but sit looking at the water, hating what Cody Morse has done to me even though this day he himself has done nothing. But circumstance has made him plow under the best day in years, burying promise under the muddy past.

I try to calm myself by watching seagulls swoop and dive against a hazy sky. Below, wave after wave breaks on the shore and I attempt comfort in the predictability of the roll and spew. Life is more than my little upset, I remind myself. This is Carl's wisdom, how minuscule our individual lives, no matter the drama or hurt or even joy. Life itself is huge, and we must pull in more to gain balance. So I attempt this, thinking of the ocean's other end lapping against Japan and the islands where other people live with other lives and other hurts. Is there some Japanese professor likewise disappointed in love? Has he been pulled asunder just as he emerged?

Tomorrow is another day, I tell myself. Yes, Miss Scarlett, it is indeed, and because I do give a damn, I shall put aside the unfortunate intrusion the memory of Cody Morse triggered by our hallway encounter, and take up where I so blissfully left off. Harley Keith shall crawl into bed with me and allow his warm buttocks to press against my prick, and I shall sleep well. But positive thought cannot overpower inner turmoil and I awaken after a restless night, absent any morning erection, gut complaining at my lack of food.

I wolf down a bowl of cereal to calm the innards and skip coffee, which would rile them again. I shower and dress, thinking of Harley in class at ten. *Dare I approach him about another tryst? Will he come to me on his own? Will he be enticed by the promise of my doing things to him or will he be repelled by an old man's advances?* By the time I reach the university, it's all fused into a maelstrom and it's all Cody's fault.

In class I had planned to discuss three stories as examples of what we've been after. Harley's is one of these and while I'd planned to discuss his last, I move it to first because I need the connection. The topic is style and without naming the writer I introduce the story.

"Longing," I begin. "From the first sentence we gain a sense of longing. We are never told Michael is longing but we see by his actions that he is bereft, almost grieving in his need of love."

And here I begin to read. I've already read the story countless times just to be with Harley because he is within the words. I glance at him now and see him riveted, as if he's never heard his work aloud. Maybe he hasn't. We should do that. I could tutor him.

Discussion about the story is lively. Harley offers nothing while I sneak a couple of smiles his way and prod the discussion until I've gotten as much as I can from the class. Reluctantly I move to the next. It gets half the effort and the third still less. When class ends and they all start to leave, I fix on Harley who remains seated. My heart leaps. I am in ecstasy, reborn, saved. *Hallelujah!*

"How are you doing?" I ask as I go to him.

He shrugs. "I dunno."

"Not man trouble again."

"Still."

"Ah, I see." But of course I don't. I thought he was done with the shitheel. "You're back together, then?"

"Not quite." He shakes his head. "It's kind of a mess. You know how things can get."

Here I purposely pause, hoping he'll pick up on what he's doing to me, but youth is never as perceptive as age would have it. Youth is energetically oblivious, even when he's trying, and I do think Harley tries. He just can't pick up on an old man's needs.

"Would you like to talk about it? Maybe we could go some-where."

He hasn't expected this and I see hesitation, like he's embar-rassed for me. And I regret the overture, almost regret the fuck. "Of course you may have plans," I quickly add.

He thinks about it, which in itself is wounding. How can it be that he has to think? He knows what I can give him. I'll make him come buckets. We can fuck for hours—but suddenly it's Cody I'm fucking and I shake my head. "Never mind," I say as I get up so quickly the chair topples.

Harley stands. "You okay?"

"Yes, fine."

At the door he asks where we can go. He says it like it's the most casual thing on earth, which I suppose it is to him while to me it is the end all be all.

"Would you like to come to my place? Have a drink?"

"Okay."

On the drive I wonder if he even remembers us fucking. He seems much the neophyte, like he's gotten into a car with an older man for the first time in his life and he has no idea I've even got a dick or will offer it to him. I try not to speed, then try not to go too slow lest he see an elder at the wheel. At the house he tosses his backpack onto a chair and starts looking at the books that line one wall of the living room. The house is a 1924 bungalow, small, cozy, comfortable. I open wine, pour two glasses, invite him to sit, but he takes the wine and remains at the books.

"What are you looking for?" I ask.

"Something I've read," he says with a laugh.

"Give it time. You'll read them all."

I'm beside him, ecstatic with his proximity. I sip wine when I really want to get his pants down. I could fuck him standing at the books. We could recite titles as he takes my cock. "Who's your favorite author?" I ask, trying to derail myself.

"I like Hemingway's stories but not his style. Updike is good and Chabon. I don't know. I guess I'm looking for one of them to drill down into me and so far none has."

"Keep looking."

It's the second glass of wine before we settle onto the sofa and I ask him about his boyfriend. Painful as this is, it remains my sole avenue and so I listen like the wise man he expects. My arm is on the sofa's back, not quite reaching him.

As he relates a tumultuous coupling followed by abandonment followed by more coupling, he sorts out his own relationship, concluding once again that Jason is a shit. "But he's got a big dick," he adds with a wry chuckle, "and god he can fuck."

"I suppose you have to decide, then, what it is you want. Love or fucking."

"Can't I have both?"

"Not always."

"Have you had that?" he asks with genuine curiosity. I look into his eyes, grateful that he wants to know anything about me at all.

"Yes, I was very much loved in a twenty-six-year relationship. He was older and died four years ago. I miss him to this day."

"Tell me about him," Harley says, taking more wine. "I need to hear something good about a man." And so I bring Carl to life for us, sharing the sex and the love, the mishaps and the joys, and during this Harley scoots in, working himself into the crook of my arm. And as I relate some of Carl's wisdom, I unzip the boy's pants and free his stiff cock. I smear his juice down the shaft and fondle him until he utters a "please," then lies back. I bend to take him into my mouth and as I suck the come from him, I know I'm at the precipice all over again, my life in these young hands. *Maybe he will remain*, I think, as I taste his spunk.

IMAGINATION MORPHS INTO REALITY

Doug Harrison

The tropical noonday sun forced its way through my closed
eyelids. Or was it intuition that woke me from a dreamy
slumber to scan the Hawaiian surf? No matter. I raised myself
on my elbows, conscious of my eager hard-on straining painfully against the metal and leather confines of my cock cage—
deliciously decadent on a family beach. He was standing waist
deep in shimmering, sea-green water, staring at me. I grinned,
he smiled. He was too far away for me to scrutinize his facial
features, but I sensed he was handsome. And what a body, at
least the upper half: broad shoulders, very broad indeed; well-
sculpted biceps; a strong chest and clearly defined pecs whose
cleavage pointed to classic washboard abs. I'd read that women
are most attracted to great abs. If so, he could have any woman
on the beach.

But he was still staring at me. Me! He reached under the
water and appeared to adjust his swimsuit. Board shorts?
Trunks? Speedos? A bikini? A thong? He answered my query

by turning, jumping and diving into an oncoming wave. What a butt! At least from a distance. Not a bubblebutt, but solid muscle held prisoner by a white bikini. He disappeared for a few disappointing but teasing seconds and popped up in a quiet trough beyond the breaking waves. Then, with powerful strokes, he swam in my direction, parallel to the shore. Again he stood, now nipple deep. His smile broadened, if such were possible, and he dove into the tumbling surf. He emerged facing me directly, foaming water surging about his knees. He shook shimmering droplets from his light brown hair and torso, which was covered with a fine coat of brown wisps. Not overly hairy, mind you, but just enough to accentuate his masculinity, strong but gentle. A gold ring swung from each nipple. His left earlobe sported a similar ring.

Online ads for white and yellow racing bikinis often carry the warning that such apparel becomes transparent when wet, an enticement to buy a jock, perhaps, but certainly not for the shy. My Adonis was anything but that. The suit clung to him like a second skin. His long dick stretched from his pelvic bone almost to his hip, leaving no doubt whatsoever that he was circumcised. Two drawstrings fell over the edge of the suit, and their ends curled around the base of his balls, which were tightly cupped by the pouch's lower contours. They were large, at least in my book, and they hadn't contracted much, if at all. I stared. What's a boy to do?

I fantasized kneeling in front of him, sliding his suit over his hairy legs—he steps out of it, his dick springs to attention, my mouth closes over his balls, perhaps urging them all the way in with my hands if necessary; slack jaw and pursed lips are a staple of my repertoire. And then teasing his balls with my tongue and a slight tug of my head while running my fingers over his dick prior to stroking it. And, finally, oh, yes, taking that dick in my mouth, grabbing his hips, pulling him into me, all the way in, burying my nose in his crotch fur.

My cock pulsed and ached, testing the limits of my cock cage.

He strode toward me, his pace a delicate and perhaps deliberate balance between eager jog and contained lope. I sat up. My butt plug provided a gentle but insistent reminder of its presence. He halted at the edge of our large rainbow blanket and scrutinized me, hands across his chest, his dick also throbbing. I guess I looked embarrassed, but hopeful. What, me a tease? What would Daddy think?

My visitor relaxed with his hands behind his back, probably resting on his gorgeous butt. His posture reminded me of a hunk leaning against a lamppost, but there was no pole to support him, just firm muscle. He slid into a seductive pose from which the slightly concave curvature of his torso emerged. I'd heard that some guys have eight-packs, but I was more than grateful to worship the six-pack hunk appraising me. A furrow ran from his pecs to his navel, bisecting his torso, and heightened his abs. I puffed out my chest.

"Aloha, I'm Craig." His voice was a perfect fit to a perfect body, a resonant baritone, secure in cadence and measured in tone. He knelt on his haunches and held out his hand. I didn't hesitate, drawn by his humongous biceps, and reached over to him, expecting a bone-crunching grasp, but was rewarded with a firm yet tender, almost enticing grip. Was I reading too much into this encounter? Well, he did approach me. Now what to do? I felt like a fisherman who had snagged a marlin almost too large for his small boat. Craig was about ten years older than my twenty-five. Let him take the lead.

This *aloha* business still felt strange, but I went for it anyway. "Aloha, I'm Jim," I replied, and smiled. I breathed deeply and drifted into his salt-water aroma. He wasn't trailing seaweed, but he sure did smell like the ocean, with a hint of sweet brine, a fragrance. I longed to lick him dry, linger at the pleats of his chest muscles, lick his pits and burrow between his asscheeks. My mind conjured an image of him staked out on the hot sand, four limbs pulled taut, struggling, straining, his dick pointing to the heavens as I stroked myself into a glorious release....

"Boy Jim, I gather," Craig said, looking at my glistening collar of polished stainless steel links secured by a padlock. I nodded.

Craig glanced at the torso-shaped indent in our blanket. "Where's Daddy?"

"Taking a leak."

"He's got himself one hell of a good-looking boy. Cute, and a great body."

"Thanks."

"You're a few inches shorter than me, and wiry like a male model—not the beefy Charles Atlas type, more like someone from *Physique Pictorial*. Where did those muscles come from?"

"I'm a gymnast."

"I could have guessed. With a little weight lifting thrown in to keep in tone?"

"Yep."

"Like bench presses, flys, pullovers."

"Yep."

Craig waited.

"And a few more," I offered with a shrug. "Curls, raises, and crunches and sit-ups. And yoga to keep limber."

I paused, then added, "Looks like you've been through the drill."

"Yeah, but you're something else. Wish I had my camera."

I blushed, although my flush probably didn't show through my freckles and ruddy skin. My father was a redhead, and I carried on the family tradition, although my hair was closely cropped into a crew cut, unlike the few strands Dad combed and carefully, indeed artistically, draped over his forehead. My time would come, but, for now, I'd make the most of my good looks.

Craig looked over my shoulder.

"Putting the make on my boy?" I heard Daddy ask. I couldn't see if he wore a frown or a smirk.

"Just getting acquainted," Craig answered, standing to his full height, which about matched Daddy's six-one.

"So I see," Daddy said, glancing at Craig's crotch. He pushed his hand forward.

The two men shook, and Craig winced. Daddy left no doubt as to who was in charge, but tempered his authority with an invitation.

"I'm Glen," Daddy said, and added, "pull up your towel."

"I'm Craig. Yeah, I'd like to." He glanced at me, turned and jogged off.

Daddy put his hands on his hips and stared down at me. Great bod, but far, far too much was hidden by his baggy blue nylon surfer board shorts. And good grief—he wouldn't know which end of a surfboard to push into the water. He's an engineer and could quickly figure it out. But mounting it? Ha!

"So, my boy's been flirting, huh?" Daddy asked as he cuffed my shoulder.

"Well…er…I…uh, well, he came over here. Sir!"

"With an encouraging come-hither look from you?"

I counted my toes.

"It's okay, boy. If you're gonna fish, catch a good one. And you did." He plopped down and stretched out beside me. I lay back and snuck a quick peek at my chest and stomach, which looked exceptionally delineated at this sharp angle. Daddy put his forearm under my neck and pulled himself closer to me. Goose bumps erupted as his torso slid along mine, despite his shorts. He tugged on my collar. "Whatever happens, you're my boy—you know that—but occasionally I like to share." He paused. "With the right person."

Jesus, I thought, *so now I'm a boy toy. Well, I still have one aperture unplugged.* I licked my lips.

Daddy closed his eyes. I admired his body for the umpteenth time. My Daddy! Fuck! Holy fuck! Bristles of black hair pushed through his shaved torso; he still modeled and "acted" in porn videos, even at his age. He delighted in my giggles whenever he lowered himself onto my body and playfully slithered his scratchy chest over mine before fucking me hard. Like Craig, he had great abs, and his muscles stood out in a heavy bas-relief: three horizontal lines cut across his trunk, announcing a six-pack from hell and accentuating his obliques. He wore his thick black hair on the longish side, and I loved to see him shake his head as he peered through uncooperative strands when he procrastinated over a much-needed hair cut. Square jaw, Aquiline nose. A five o'clock shadow that appeared about three p.m. Long legs firm from years of running, mostly track and around our flat town, not much hill work—which was obvious from his great calves, but his thighs needed gym persuasion.

We're both athletic, although we focus on different activities. And we're pretty well matched otherwise—sharp technical minds; we both joke a lot, are partial to puns but tend to be deep thinkers. Our coffee table and bedside tables are piled with scientific mags and journals, and, I must admit, sci-fi, adventure, and spy novels. The trait we have most in common is the love we have for each other, a spiritual marriage I can feel but not explain, a match of beautiful bodies and beautiful minds.

Craig approached with a white beach towel draped over his shoulder. Daddy motioned him to the far side of the blanket. Craig positioned his towel contiguous to Daddy's side of the blanket and stretched out. Two hard-ons out of three wasn't bad, and just maybe there was a third one under those damn board shorts.

"So, where are you from?" Daddy asked Craig.

"Born and raised in upper state New York. Good place to leave behind. I prefer warm weather, so I made my way to California."

"And your line of work," Daddy pressed on, "if I may ask?"

"Oh, sure, I'm a personal fitness coach and a masseur. Have a space here in Kona where I see clients, some on a regular basis, some vacationers. Also go to other islands, Kauai and Maui, once a month."

"So that's why you're so buffed."

"Yeah, I have to set a good example—can't be a chef who won't sample his own creations."

Daddy raised an eyebrow and cocked his head.

"Yeah," Craig offered, "sometimes I give more than a massage."

"What's your client base?"

"Oh, the cross section is pretty even—young, old, men and women."

Daddy raised himself to a sitting position. "And which side of the pond do you fish in?"

Craig threw his head back and laughed. "Both sides."

Daddy relaxed with his arms underneath his head.

"So, what's your line of work?" Craig asked as he scanned Daddy's body.

"Engineer, somewhat specialized." His eyes locked onto

Craig's and they swam in each other's gaze. "I pull a few hours from a hectic Silicon Valley schedule to make it to the gym with forays to the track, especially on weekends—I enjoy long, solitary runs." Daddy smiled and Craig threw him a thumbs-up.

I scowled.

Just then two girls, or should I say young ladies, sauntered by. They weren't the *Playboy* Bunny type, but close enough. They wore matching orange string bikinis, covering their crotches but not their butts. Not too bad for a woman. Their halter thingies covered their nipples, but just barely. Craig watched them closely, but Daddy couldn't care less. They were gym toned, with small but well-defined biceps, a smattering of ab development, and firm thighs, and probably entered physique contests. What was going on? A freakin' convention? A nearby body building competition? Well, I guess the well-heeled pot-bellied, bald business execs and their overweight, bejeweled wives with beehive hairdos claimed some other portion of the beach—like unto like. The Amazons looked toward us, giggled, linked arms and ran into the water.

"Are we supposed to follow?" Daddy teased.

"You won't keep up with them in those balloon pants," I snapped.

"All right, wise-ass," Daddy said, and stood. He untied his drawstring with a fluid motion. Then he teased his long Velcro fly open, reveling in the staccato crackle he orchestrated. Finally, ever so slowly, he lowered his shorts. The top of a black Speedo appeared. Next the crotch. Then his knees.

"Go *haole,* go!" A cluster of Hawaiian teenage boys hooted and threw Daddy a shaka.

He lowered his clown pants to the ground, stepped out and tossed them onto our pile of clothes.

"Satisfied?" he beamed.

My "Yes, Sir!" and Craig's "Yeah!" were an impromptu off-key duet.

Daddy did a half turn and faced the boys, arms akimbo.

"You're a walking gym ad," one shouted.

"Mahalo," Daddy answered, and turned back to us.

Daddy hadn't shaved his legs—his last "appearance" didn't require it—and his leg fur turned me on, as usual. A tuft of black hair rose from the rear of his suit, reaching for the small of his back.

He kicked my leg. "Roll over," he ordered, "it's your turn."

"Daddiee," I whined.

"No arguments," he said. "Do it now."

I complied. Slowly. Craig raised himself onto his elbow. "Good goddamn, he's wearing a thong."

My entire body blushed.

"What a motherfuckin' bubblebutt," Craig said. "And stripes! A great caning job—well spaced and even on both sides. More surprises in this little family."

Daddy swatted both my cheeks with his palms, and none too gently.

"Yeouch," I yelled, and jumped into a crouch.

"I see the outlines of a butt plug," Craig announced.

"Yep," said Daddy. "He takes a medium thong and a large butt plug. Hard to dress."

"Jesus Christ!" I pounded my fists into the blanket.

"He loves the attention," Craig hooted.

"You've got his number," Daddy shot back.

"I'd like to get something else from him," Craig said. I turned my head to catch his wink. Almost threw my neck out of joint. Hard work, this being a boy toy.

"His body really turns me on: those wide, defined, *V*-shaped trapezius muscles... like a stingray," he snickered, and droned on, theatrically, "the narrow hips, the ass from hell, enough to drive any man crazy. Great legs, too. I love the light blond fuzz."

"Don't pop your britches," Daddy guffawed.

"I've already stained them—I'm a dribbler. Particularly with a live centerfold."

That did it! I hopped to my feet.

"I'm not a freakin' object," I yelled with clenched fists.

"No, an objet d'art," Craig said with soothing tones. "I've never seen such physical perfection in a boy. And a sharp mind to boot, I'll venture."

"*Mais oui,*" Daddy nodded with a mischievous smirk. "That's why I corralled him. A smart, frisky colt."

Oh, god, I was really feeling the cage now. My engorged cock ached against its leather and metal confines. I rubbed my crotch.

Daddy swatted my hand, pulled Craig toward him, and forced us into a tight circle.

"Lower your thong, boy," he ordered.

"Daddy, pleeez!" I whinnied.

"Just the front. No one will notice."

Craig put his arms over my shoulders and peered at my crotch.

"We're waiting," Daddy said.

I looked around. No one was watching. The boys had left. The two girls were off in Lesbo Land somewhere, I guessed. So I did it. My cock sprang up to my belly, cage and all, and landed with a *thwap*. My dickhead, covered with precum, strained and pulsed against the cage's cylindrical tip. We all three stared at it.

"Clean yourself, boy," Daddy ordered, and I caught Craig's leer. I stuck my index finger into the end of my penis prison and

swiped the tip of my cock. I hesitated. *Where to wipe my finger?*
Daddy solved my conundrum.

"Lick it clean!"

Well, it's not like I hadn't done this before. My finger flew in
and out of my mouth at record speed, and then my hand disappeared behind my back.

"Not done yet," Daddy barked. I blanched.

"Mind if I finish the job?" Craig asked.

Daddy raised his eyebrows a tad and replied with a thumbs-
up. I took a deep breath and relaxed. *Oh, boy!*

Craig squeezed, pushed, and rotated three fingers into the
cage. His fingernails were trimmed to the quick. He massaged
my dickhead, languorously withdrew his hand, raised it to his
mouth, smiled and leisurely cleaned his fingers, a contented cat
grooming himself.

"Good-tasting boy," Craig said to Daddy, not even looking
at me. I bit my lip.

"Let's take a quick dip and head back to our room," Daddy
suggested. "We're here at the Guiltmore for the rest of the
week." He winked and nudged Craig, who replied, "Sure. Hot
damn!" perhaps a bit too vigorously.

"Pull up your pants, boy," Daddy commanded. Which I did.
Like, fast. Daddy and Craig stood on each side of me; we all
linked arms and ran into the waves. Well, they sorta carried
me. But I didn't give a damn who saw my ass. After all, it had
been anointed a bubblebutt. I would've wiggled it at any nosy
onlookers, had there been any; seagulls didn't count.

They dropped me in waist-deep water. I stood with my arms
folded across my chest.

"Com'on, boy, enjoy the water," Daddy cajoled.

"Uh, I'll catch up. I'll just take it one drop at a time."

Craig grabbed Daddy's arm. They disappeared into a wave

like two frolicking dolphins, black-clad butt and white-clad butt, yin and yang. They emerged on the other side of the crest, put their arms around each other, and sunk from view. *What the hell is going on down there?* Well, it couldn't last too long. Craig popped up, his suit at midthigh, gulped some air and sank from view. Next Daddy rose, floating on his stomach, his suit also inappropriately placed. His tan torso, which played counterpoint with his bobbing white butt, glistened in the noonday sun, each droplet of water a small prism that captured the light and scattered it into minuscule rainbows. Two arms appeared around his waist, and he pumped his ass a few times before he jackknifed. The water churned as arms, legs and torsos swirled like intertwined pinwheels. A large wave plunged over them and they burst through the surface, sputtering, and stood in crotch-deep water. Their suits were still midthigh, and two hard dicks pointed at each other as they bobbed in and out of the receding wave. They threw back their heads and howled. Then they wrapped their arms about each other and kissed while reluctantly but diligently tugging each other's suits to respectable, responsible positions, though two bulges remained more than evident. *Can their inseams tolerate any more abuse?* I turned and slogged back to the blanket.

I sat and locked my arms around my bent knees. *I like to watch Daddy grooving with a woman or two at a party, maybe even pumpin' pussy, but that's just play. This man-to-man stuff is scary. I didn't know Daddy could be attracted to older men. He's stepping out of his role—jeez—maybe it just is a role. Like, is he a real Daddy? Gosh, he has to follow his heart, but can it be away from me?*

The two men lunged through knee-deep water and marched across the shallows. They were holding hands and laughing as they ran up to me. I stared uncertainly at them. Daddy sat and draped his arm around my neck. I shrugged. Daddy glanced at Craig, who stood with his hands at his side.

"Craig, move your towel over there," he requested.

Craig moved quickly to comply. He sat on his repositioned towel and draped his arm around my other shoulder. I took a deep breath, looked at Daddy, over to Craig and back at Daddy.

What's with me?

Prickly fingers were kneading my stomach, just like before a final exam I wasn't prepared for. Only now my abdomen was a cauldron sending flashes of hot fire throughout my body.

Don't I even get a vote? Guess not. I'm not Daddy's slave—I didn't sign a contract giving him absolute authority and power. Still, I'm his boy—I passed my qualifying exams long ago. And we discuss lots of things, like picking TV shows, even coming here. He must've really fallen for Craig. Shit! Guess I'll just gave to play along and see what happens. Fuck! Do I really have any choice?

Daddy rested his free hand on my knee. "It's okay, boy."

Craig withdrew his hand, folded his palms in his lap and lowered his head.

"I should leave," he mumbled.

I looked over at him. Aside from Daddy, he was the only man I had met who possessed the sublime mixture of passion, compassion and beauty I desired. He wore his selfless mantle well, even in wet, skimpy Speedos, no regal robes required.

"Don't leave," I whispered. *Now what?* Then, like the chorus from Verdi's *Nabucco*, "Fly thought, on golden wings," a compelling concept rose to my consciousness.

"Daddy's love, my love, yeah, like…like our love, can grow to include others," I mumbled *sotto voce*.

Craig and Daddy looked at each other.

"Let's hightail it to our room and explore this situation," Daddy suggested. I stood. Craig slowly rose and hugged me, tentative at first, but I melded into him and he squeezed the breath from me.

Daddy stepped into his clown pants, I slid into my beach bum shorts and Craig wrapped his towel around his waist. We packed our crap and hiked back to our condo, swaggering as close as our paraphernalia would allow, but with no hands free to clutch and swing. We passed under tall palm trees, all trimmed to a fair-thee-well and coconut-free, of course, to protect the tourists, past lush, manicured gardens with a panoply of plants, none of which I recognized, except orchids and huge white and yellow trumpet bushes.

We provoked a few stares, but so fuckin' what? I was escorted by two gorgeous hunks, perfect candidates for Buckingham Palace Guards. A thought surfaced: *Some Daddies have a stable of boys; can a boy have more than one Daddy?*

We scuttled across the lobby and past the SHIRTS REQUIRED sign. Daddy forced a closing elevator door open, and we squeezed into the crowded lift, our backs and chests sporting a few droplets of water and stubborn grains of sand, to a few "Humpfs." *Tough shit, prim and proper prudes!* We added our masculine aroma to a metallic shell that imprisoned the stench of perfume, aftershave, and aloha shirts drenched with perspiration and cigar smoke.

"Eight, please," Daddy requested.

No one moved.

Craig jostled his way to the floor panel, pushed the requisite button, squared his shoulders—and his towel slid to the floor. A gasp. A chuckle. Craig flexed his back muscles, reached to retrieve the towel and draped it over his shoulders. More than one woman stared at his crotch when he turned. We arrived at eight and scuttled into the hallway. A man started to disembark before a shrill voice stopped him: "No dear, let's go to nine and walk down." We clomped into our room and cracked up.

Daddy stepped out of his board shorts, I grabbed Craig's towel and then hopped out of my shorts before hanging them in the bathroom to dry.

"Beer?" Daddy asked Craig.

"Goes through me so fast I'll have to pee straightaway."

"It's okay, boy will take care of you," Daddy replied as he glanced my way. I raised one eyebrow as I fetched a diet soda.

"Bottoms up!" Daddy toasted. Both men looked at me. I lowered my head to hide my smile. Overeagerness can be a bottom's bane. Daddy spread a large white fluffy towel on the couch and perched. I sat next to him while Craig sneered at a piss elegant wing chair and sprawled on the rug.

"So, Jim. How did you get into this boy business?"

I put my soda down and snuggled closer to Daddy.

"I grew up in New England. Went to school in Boston. Majored in physics. I enjoyed mechanics and thermo a lot, so I stayed an extra year and took a double major in M.E.—mechanical engineering, that is."

Craig raised his eyebrows. "I knew you were one smart guy."

"Yeah, thanks."

"And sexy as hell to boot," Craig added, as he stroked himself.

I mimicked his stroking motions and continued.

"With that background I didn't have any trouble landing a job in the aerospace industry, so, like Daddy, I came west."

Craig focused on my collar.

"Yeah, well, I went the straight route in high school, discovered guys in college, or, should I say, to be politically correct, explored my sexuality."

We all laughed.

"Some interesting fags are to be found in frat houses. And, surreptitiously, gay porn. I saw one of Daddy's flicks. His scenes were fodder for many of my JO sessions. I decided to track him down after I graduated."

"How the hell did you do *that*?" Craig asked.

"After passing courses in advanced math and relativistic quantum mechanics, it was no sweat. I just sent a fan letter to one of the companies he worked for. With a few pictures thrown in."

We all laughed.

"And the rest is history," Daddy concluded.

"I'll drink to that," Craig said as he downed the rest of his beer. Daddy and I followed suit. "Let's watch the sunset."

We stepped onto the balcony and plunked our drinks on the ledge. I stood between Daddy and Craig, and we wrapped our arms around each other's waists as the bottom of the setting sun kissed the distant waterline. Sailboats, skiffs and fishing boats made their way to the local pier. A few het couples carrying blankets and small coolers passed below us, headed for the beach and hanky-panky, most likely. Daddy's gaze trailed them into the shadows.

"What was your most interesting experience as a masseur?" Daddy asked Craig.

Craig replied without hesitation. "It was with a young married couple, both good looking. Sharp, too, judging by the way they negotiated my fee. I fucked her while he watched, then I fucked him while she watched. They had a camcorder going." Craig paused for dramatic effect. "Then he fucked her in the ass doggie-style while I screwed him doggie-style. Quite the arrangement. I was actually pushing him deep into her."

"Probably work with three guys," Daddy said.

"Oh, sure," Craig answered.

He leaned over and placed his elbows on the ledge, stretched his lanky legs, and crossed his ankles. The dim light cast shadows among the ridges of his taut quads and hamstrings. I fumbled with my drink as I fought the urge to kneel between him and the railing, scratched knees and back notwithstanding, yank his suit down until his boner whacked me in the face, and service his big dick.

Daddy stepped behind me, placed his palms on the ledge, and captured me scissor-like with his hips.

Craig scanned the peaceful vista.

"Beautiful," he said. "I always enjoy this view."

We rested in silence as the sun slid farther below the horizon.

"Perhaps we'll be lucky enough to see a green flash," Craig said.

Daddy lowered my thong. I forced my legs farther apart so I could feel the wet surface twisting the hair as he tugged away. Daddy lowered his own suit. His long, hard dick pressed into my buttcrack.

"Ever see a blue flash?" I asked as I backed more into Daddy.

"Nope, not lucky enough," Craig answered.

Daddy began a gentle pumping motion.

"Very rare, even on a clear night," Craig added.

I gasped, not an announcement of gained scientific insight, but an appreciation of raw, rutting sex.

Craig looked our way.

"We should go inside," he urged. "We're not the only ones watching the sunset."

True, the balconies on either side of ours held chatty couples whom I hadn't noticed. It was dark by now, and we went indoors without pulling up our suits. A gentle breeze wafted in from the ocean.

"Let's go into the bathroom, Sirs," I suggested, hoping I wasn't being too forward.

"Okay, Sir boy," Daddy replied. His grin would have shamed the Cheshire cat.

They followed me into the bathroom.

"Time for our shower. Will three guys fit in there?" Craig asked.

"Not yet," I replied. "Face each other."

"Well, well," Craig said.

I put my hands on their shoulders and nudged them closer. They pressed into each other and linked hands. I grabbed a gigantic white towel and swiped their backs simultaneously. They moaned and groaned when I wiped their asses and legs. I paused. Then I knelt and buried my face in Daddy's crack.

"Jesus," he said.

I burrowed deeper and used my teeth to tug on a few hairs. I ran my tongue around his hole and pushed in as far as possible, which wasn't too deep since he was standing, but I did my best. My efforts were appreciated, judging by Daddy's purring.

I withdrew, uttered a slow "Yummy," licked my lips, and crawled around to Craig. I went to work on his muscular ass. *At last!* I nibbled each orb and did my best to make him purr as well. I succeeded and stood.

"Now for the front. Face me," I ordered. They followed instructions okay—for Daddies.

I wiped their chests, pinching a nipple or two through the fluffy towel. Then I squatted and blew on their dicks as I daubed their crotches and worked my way down to their toes.

"Feels great," Daddy said.

"Yeah," Craig added, "real good."

Their dicks reflected their delight. And their asses looked fantastic in the mirror. I tossed the towel to one side.

Daddy looked me in the eye. "Kneel," he ordered.

I opened my mouth and took his dick. I could tell he wanted to pee before he got real hard.

"I know you can take two dicks, boy. But can you take two pissing dicks?" he asked.

"Christ almighty," Craig said.

I pulled the edge of my mouth as far wide as I could with my index finger, and Daddy guided Craig's dick into me. I clamped down softly.

Daddy put his arm around Craig's waist and Craig followed suit. Then Daddy started. Just a few drops. Likewise, Craig. Daddy's flow increased and so did Craig's.

I held my head back, throat open, and gulped as fast as I could. Finally, my eyes must have bulged, 'cause Daddy said, "That's enough, let's finish in the toilet." I sank back on the floor, their piss sloshing in my stomach.

They shook their dicks and stared at me. "Great job, boy!" Daddy said. Craig concurred. "Water?" Daddy asked.

"No, thanks," I answered and licked my lips. My cock cage pointed straight up.

"Stay in here until summoned," I said in a mock gruff tone as I scampered into the bedroom and closed the door. I didn't know what they'd do, but I sure knew where I was headed. I donned an outfit and oiled my body. An enormous mirror hung above the breakfront that stretched along the wall facing the king-sized four-poster bed. I lit an emergency hurricane lamp, fluffed up four bed pillows, and doused the overhead lights. An eerie, seductive glow pervaded the room.

I crouched in the corner.

"Come in," I said in a seductive tone. "But first turn off the bathroom light."

The door opened.

"Holy shit!" Craig exclaimed.

Daddy chuckled. "Guess we belong on the bed."

I crawled over to the dresser and pushed the start button on my iPod. Disco music filled the room.

I grasped the footboard and slowly rose as I leaned back, knowing full well that they could see the amorphous reflection of my flexed back muscles in the mirror.

Daddy and Craig were embedded in the pillows, hands across their chests. They applauded when they saw my bare chest and Daddy's surfer shorts. I lowered the waistband until the top of my red thong peeked out, and rubbed my taut abdomen.

"Take it off, take it off," they yelled.

I pulled my shorts back up.

I did a full turn and grabbed one of the six-foot-tall bedposts, humped it in time to the raucous beat, and lowered my shorts. I caressed the crotch of my thong; the outline of my cock cage was clearly delineated. I pranced, stepped out of the shorts, and threw them a kiss. I did a half turn, leaned my bare ass into the footboard, wiggled it, slid back to my ersatz pole, pulled myself partway up, locked my legs around the slippery wood, and gyrated. The applause was deafening in our small room. Finally, I hopped onto the bed and seductively lowered my thong, which I kicked into Craig's face. I stood motionless, hands on hips, in a bulging black posing strap, its thin white strings climbing over the natural curves of my hips and disappearing into my butt-crack. More applause accompanied hoots and hollers. I did a backflip off the bed, landed on my feet, and finished my performance with a wild dance, replete with turns, kicks and side-steps. The music stopped as I did a split, legs flat on the floor, with my disembodied shit-eatin' grin above the headboard.

There was no immediate applause. My audience was too busy wanking. I turned up the room light a tad and disappeared into the kitchen.

I returned naked, except for my cock cage, with three cans of soda. Craig and Daddy slid apart and I slithered between them.

"Great show, my beautiful boy," Daddy chuckled.

"Yeah," Craig said. "Such a beauty."

We drank in silence.

Daddy raised his index finger to his chin. "On your knees boy, facing the headboard," he ordered.

"Yes Sir!"

Daddy fluffed the pillow between me and the headboard.

"All right if Craig fucks you?" he asked.

"Er, yes, Sir," I replied, not wanting to appear overeager as my cock stiffened again.

"Good! And I'll fuck Craig. Okay?"

"Okay."

Both men put on rubbers and Craig lubed my hole while Daddy greased Craig's. There was some finger poking and prodding, but not much was needed for two hungry, greedy cavities. I was glad for short, smooth fingernails. Craig and I spread our legs.

And then it began. Oh, yeah! The fuck of my life.

Craig knelt and pushed his way into me. I took all of his long dick and he flopped onto my back, his arms on either side of me, push-up style. He grunted as Daddy entered him slowly, pulled back slightly, pushed in a bit more, pulled back again and then with a mighty shove made it all the way in. Craig yelped. Daddy must've plopped onto Craig's back, 'cause Craig felt heavier.

Daddy started a slow pump, Craig followed, and I inched

forward. I couldn't decide if I should brace myself or go with the flow. I relaxed and went where two sweaty, grunting hunks propelled me, which was into the pillow. I grabbed the head-board and pushed back and forced Craig's dick deeper into me, which had a chain reaction effect on Daddy's dick.

"Ride 'em, cowboy!" Craig hooted.

"Fuck me, Sirs, oh, yeah, fuck this boy good, real good!" I screamed.

"You got it, boy!" Daddy answered and threw his weight into Craig.

"Oh shit, I'm coming," Craig howled. "I'm gonna fill your boy up."

"I'm with you!" Daddy bayed.

"Yeah, dump your load in me, big Daddy!" Craig answered with a final thrust. I swear I could feel his condom swelling in me. He collapsed onto my back, panting, and our perspiration joined into a slippery puddle—which only made him slide farther along my back with Daddy's final heave.

"Jesus!" Daddy bellowed. He paused, pulled out with a pop and collapsed onto his back. Craig followed. The two men lay side by side, perpendicular to me, breathing hard. I turned and lay facedown next to them, sweaty and sore, and reveled in my bliss.

Daddy got up and brought us each a bottle of fresh water. We gulped in contented silence.

"Your boy hasn't come yet," Craig announced.

Daddy retrieved a key and handed it to Craig. We both stood, me stock-still. Craig knelt in front of me, finally figured out my cage's lock and clasp arrangement, fumbled with the lock and unfastened the strap that circumscribed my cock and balls. Then he slowly, ever so carefully pulled the cage off. Daddy watched the entire process. His smile broadened and he pleasured himself as Craig completed each step.

Craig threw the cage onto the bed, put his hands around my hips and drew me into his mouth—not with a slow, deliberate, teasing motion, but rapidly, greedily, insistently. No complaints from me. And this was the best way yet to view those shoulders and biceps. I grabbed the back of his head. Daddy straddled Craig's ass and latched on to my nipples, knowing only too well what I needed, what I craved. Craig laved my dickhead and shaft with copious spit, in, out, in, out, and Daddy matched Craig's motions with tit pinching and pulling. It didn't take long.

I spurted. And I continued to spurt through spasm after spasm. Because I was young. Because it had been so long. Because I wanted this man. And Craig took it all, took my essence, drew my boyhood into him.

I screamed "Daddy," and then clutched Craig in my crotch as I softened and my breathing subsided. I let go and he sat cross-legged in front of me. I leaned over and ran my fingers through his hair, a gentle caress of deep appreciation. Daddy stepped to the side and kissed me.

I folded back into the bed, feet hanging over the side, and Craig joined me. Daddy reached for the bottles of water. I took one with trembling hands.

"No, thanks," Craig said. "I want to savor this boy as long as I can." He ran his tongue languidly around his lips.

Daddy nodded and drained his bottle. He leaned against the dresser and gazed at us.

"You make a nice couple," he said.

My eyes widened.

"Thanks," Craig said.

Silence hung in the air, not threatening, somehow welcoming. Finally, Daddy spoke in a unique, melodious flow of dulcet tones.

"I'd like Craig to be your Hawaii Daddy. And I have to go away on business in two months. Perhaps Craig can come to California and keep an eye on you. How's that sit with both of you?"

Craig and I locked eyes. "Great. Very great," Craig said.

"Yes, Sir," I answered.

We remained motionless for a few seconds, absorbing our new situation.

Craig broke the silence.

"Can I give your boy a bracelet that matches his collar?"

Daddy looked at me. My eyes said yes.

"We'd both like that," Daddy said. He drew Craig into a bear hug with me between them. I was glad I was shorter, so they wouldn't see yet another shit-eatin' grin. And a solitary, salty tear.

Yes, a boy can have two Daddies.

MEN OF THE OPEN ROAD

Landon Dixon

I was only a mile out of town when the first car stopped.

It was a Benz, the driver a businessman in a flawless pin-striped suit and flashy pink tie. He had rings on his fingers, his white hair was perfectly coiffed, soft and flowing; his green eyes smiled into mine. For a guy over fifty, his face was smooth and young looking, though tanned a golden brown.

"Where you headed?" he asked, as I filled the open passenger-side window with my blond-haired head and broad, bare shoulders. Ignoring the ringing of his cell phone, he looked me over.

"West," I responded vaguely.

"Then get in. I'm headed out to my cottage. I can take you about thirty miles down the road."

"Sounds good," I said, and pulled the door open and slid into the leather bucket seat next to him.

His cologne was a little on the heavy side, but I put up with it. He went on and on about the pressures of his job, how his trophy wife was a royal pain in the ass, until I put a stop to it—by placing my hand over his crotch.

He'd had a bulge in his pinstripes ever since I'd gotten into the luxury car. And now I covered it with a warm, smooth palm, working his erection bigger and thicker by rubbing up and down. He groaned and gripped the steering wheel, looking at me with slightly glazed eyes.

"My wife...I don't..."

"Sure you do," I said, gripping his dick through the expensive cloth and stroking. "Fuck your wife. She's nothing but a pain in the ass, anyway, remember?"

He forgot all about his wife and the pressures of his job as I rubbed the rather impressive length of his hard-on. I had one going in my own tight jeans that he couldn't help but notice. He reached over and reciprocated, like I knew he would, grasping my bulging cock with a manicured brown hand and squeezing and stroking.

I leaned back in the padded seat and groaned. I like older men, like them to do things to me, like doing things to them. And this aging pretty boy knew just how to show a kid a third of his age a good time with his hand.

We had our cocks out and cuddled in our bare fists by the time we were two more miles down the road. The silver fox introduced himself as Roger, while he introduced me to a pulsating erection as smooth and slick as the man himself. He liked my eight inches of meat, too, judging by the way he clutched and pulled.

The white lines whizzed by, Roger's foot pressing harder and harder on the gas, as we tugged faster and faster. His prick throbbed in my hand like the motor under the hood, just as hot. I swirled up and down his length, over the top of his own fleshy hood, and he jacked my dong with his tongue hanging out and his eyes off the road. He wanted to two-hand all of my cock, but I told him, "Not at this speed."

We pumped our fists; our breath came in ragged gasps, our chests were heaving, loins thrusting up into each other's hands, pricks spearing palms. He was driving down a four-lane, separated highway, and we barely kept to our side of it.

"Fuck, kid!" Roger gasped, his cock jumping in my pistoning hand. "I'm...I'm going to..."

He came, cum rocketing out of the tip of his jacked cock, adding more pinstripes to his business attire. I milked him fast and tight and hard, and the sight of the silver-haired guy shooting sperm, his hand convulsively clenching my dick, jerked me over the edge.

"Yeah!" I grunted, bucking, jetting.

He almost forgot his own orgasm, staring at the white-hot semen geysering out of my ruptured dong. I coated that walnut dashboard and the leather seat.

"My wife won't be coming out for another day or so," he said, when he came to the turnoff to Eagle Lake. "You can stay with me—swim, boat, fish...you name it."

It was a tempting offer, since the lake was the exclusive domain of the city's elite. But I had miles to go before I slept... with anyone.

A couple of women stopped for me, intrigued by my skintight sleeveless T-shirt and blue jeans; my smooth, young, sun-bronzed body filling out the form-fitting duds. I gave them the brush and went on walking.

It was half past two and the sun was pouring gold down upon me when I was picked up by my next ride.

He was a trucker, said his name was Stu. He was driving a company big rig, his face and body grizzled from years on the road: a lean, hungry-looking fiftysomething with an iron-gray brush cut and pale-blue eyes. He stubbed out his cigarette as soon as I climbed aboard and didn't waste any time putting the rig back into gear.

"It's lonely on the road, huh?" he said.

"Yeah," I responded, liking what I saw, not so much what I was hearing. I wasn't about to become anyone's buggy buddy.

Stu was wearing a red plaid work shirt and a pair of blue nylon pants. His veiny hands on the wheel were large. That was another good sign I just couldn't ignore.

We blew through a small town in the blink of an eye and then I leaned over, unzipped him and pulled his cock out of his underwear and pants. I was not disappointed. The guy was packing a second stick shift, his meat huge and heavy in my hand, even semierect. Older men always seem to be hung.

I stroked Stu, staring into his eyes. "How 'bout we take it off-road," I offered, "and park this rig of yours in my ass?"

He shook his head, gripping the wheel with whitened knuckles. "Sure'd like to, kid. But I'm on the clock and the GPS. Can't make any stops except authorized ones."

I shrugged and leaned right over his lap, licking his gaping slit with a slurp. "No problem. Just drive, he said," I said. I swirled my wet, pink tongue around his bloated knob, then poured my plush lips over top of it.

He groaned, giving it gas, the truck leaping forward, his cock jumping harder and higher in my hand and mouth.

I dug his hairy balls out and gave them a lick. Then I gripped his sac with one hand, ringed the base of his fully erect prick with the other and dove my mouth straight down his pole until I kissed up against that second hand. His meat filled my mouth and flooded my throat, hot and throbbing, like my dick in my pants. Stu bucked on his air-cushioned seat, thrusting deep into my throat full-throttle.

I bobbed my head in rhythm to his hip movements, sucking

on his shaft, tongue stroking up and down, his cock plunging my mouth and throat. I was as hungry as he looked, smoking his pipe. He gave me a long, hard ride; then he growled and spasmed, heated salty sperm spunking my throat and mouth.

I gulped as fast as I could, not spilling a drop as Stu redlined his engine. He gave me everything he had and then more, when I released his prick in a gush of spit and hot, humid air, and he gasped, "Your turn to drive."

He knew his way around the inside of that cab like he knew his way around a man's cock. We shifted positions in no time flat, me holding the big rig steady on the road, he holding my hard-on in his hand, then his mouth.

He admired my pulsing length and breadth with his rough, sure mitt for a while, pumping slow and sensual, quick and exciting. Then he did the lean-over, inhaling my hood. He sucked hard on my cap, ravenous for meat and more meat. His head sunk lower, right down into my lap, my entire cock buried in his wet, hot maw.

I blew the horn a couple of times just to let him know I appreciated his skill. He showed me more of it, working his tongue out and over my balls. I squirmed in the seat, locked down in the man's throat, his tongue lapping at my nut sac. He pulled his head back up, plunged it back down, high-dive deep-throating me.

I clutched at his bristly hair with one hand, keeping my other sweating hand on the wheel, the road humming beneath us. He gripped my thighs, moving onto his knees on the floor now, sucking hard and long on my pipe, shifting my semen into high gear. The suction was just too intense; I couldn't hold back.

"Fuck, I'm going to come!" I warned. Then I came, bucking in the driver's seat, blowing Stu a mouth and throat full.

He took it like the hardened road-dog he was, still sucking as he swallowed, and swallowed, and swallowed.

Only afterward, when I'd softened, did he soften again. He went off on another jag about how lonely it was on the road without having anyone to ride along. I dropped off of his rig when he slowed for diesel at a station. I wasn't looking for the long haul.

A carload of young flamers skidded to a stop alongside me a few miles farther up the road, but that wasn't my speed, and I gave them the wave by.

Then a white van pulled off onto the shoulder, and I jogged on over to it. NEW DEAL MINISTRIES was stenciled on the side of the vehicle, and a man of about fifty or so was behind the wheel. He looked kindly, with his beaming brown eyes and wavy, graying hair. He had a ripe, full mouth and an angelic face, a slightly chubby body dressed in black pants and jacket and a clerical collar.

"Need a lift, my son?"

"Sure do," I responded, licking my lips.

He started in with the preaching soon after we'd exchanged names. Father Todd was part New Age and part Old Testament, counseling me on the roads that led to righteousness and the paths that led to damnation.

I stopped his proselytizing with a quick kiss to his fine mouth. His lips were soft and lush, wet from talking. He stared at me, his eyes registering official shock and condemnation, something deeper and darker in behind.

"Danny, I'm going to overlook that as—"

I kissed him again, harder, longer, speaking in tongues inside his mouth. When I broke away this time, he was panting, his face red. I told him to pull over to the side of the road so I could fuck his ass in the back of the van.

He'd had his lust frustrated for too long. He jerked the wheel over to the right and stomped on the brakes.

The first bench seat in the back was as good as any pew to worship at the man's ass. And he had a ripe, round one—smooth, pale, fleshy cheeks that quivered warm and willing under my groping hands. I smacked one, then the other, and they blushed, Todd groaning and arching his butt up at me on all fours on the seat.

The windows were tinted just dark enough so that the cars and trucks whizzing by couldn't see me baptizing the holy father's ass with my palms. I spanked him so hard that he rocked back and forth, whimpering. I was punishing him for his transgressions, and the greater transgression was yet to come.

I unzipped, pushed down my jeans and pulled out my cock, crowding in behind Todd's upraised bottom. I smacked his ass with my dong, the crack of cock-flesh against butt-flesh filling the stuffy confines of the vehicle. I bent my head down and clutched his buttocks up and bit into the right one, then the left one. The guy really did have an amazingly meaty ass, and I just couldn't get enough of it. When I licked his crack, he almost jumped right out the window.

I spread his cheeks wide and lapped at his butt cleavage, stroking wetly from his balls to his tailbone, over and over. He moaned, cheeks quivering. I speared into the delicate pink pucker of his asshole, squirming my tongue around inside, and he begged me to fuck him with my cock. He'd seen the length and the width, and his eyes had lit up with glorious anticipation.

I pulled out the tube of lube I travel with and oiled my cock. Then I slipped two slippery fingers in between Todd's thick cheeks where my tongue had just been and scrubbed his crack even slicker. He groaned, then howled, when I plugged those digits right into his anus and pumped back and forth.

The guy was tight, hot. But I was making him looser, hotter. I plowed his butt with a pistonlike motion, bouncing my fist off his buns. Then I yanked my fingers out and grabbed my cock, pushing my cap inside.

"Oh, God!" Todd yelped, calling out to his deity. "Stick it in me, Danny! Fuck my ass!"

I sunk my shaft deep into his chute, slow and steady and sensuous. His cheeks swelled before me, his anus bulging with cock. He was oven-hot and vise-tight, and I rutted around on the end of his ass, buried to the balls. He rotated his overstuffed bottom up against me, reveling in the wicked sexual sensations as much as I was.

A police car slowed down, but drove on by. It was late afternoon. Time was getting short. I had miles to go before I slept the sleep of the truly fulfilled.

I gripped Todd's waist and drew my hips slowly back, gliding my cock out of his anus. Then I lunged forward, plowing right back in again, full length, and settled into pumping the man's ass.

He gripped the seat cushion with his hands and teeth, his buttcheeks gyrating under my onslaught. I torqued up the pace even more, drilling his ass, plundering his chute. My thighs smacked so hard and so fast against his buttocks that they rippled nonstop, the sound blurring into one continuous crack.

The van rocked with our passion. Todd tore a hand off the seat and grabbed onto his cock, pulled. He bleated pure joy, instantly jacking ecstasy out of his prick and all over the seat.

I clutched his hips and pounded into his hole, my balls tattooing his butt, cock splitting his anus. I reamed him unmercifully, adding another wild orgasm to his. Sperm spewed out of the end of my sunken, shunting cock and doused the man's bowels with my superheated bliss.

I pulled out of his ass when he started crying. I pulled out of his van when he started pleading with me to stay.

I walked across the road and stuck out my thumb, looking to catch a ride or two back into town. I'm never actually trying to go anywhere. I just like getting picked up by older men and taken for rides. It's the most satisfying form of travel I know: a Daddy every day.

PROFESSOR PAPI

Randy Turk

I don't get this shit about the Daddy thing. I just don't get it. A guy who's way past fifty is considered sexy? Hot? Please. I don't like it when a younger man calls me "Daddy" online. In fact, I get downright pissed off and block those guys from talking with me again. What's up with their obsession with older guys? When I came out at nineteen, I wanted guys my age. Once my college roommate shot cum into my mouth, I knew I couldn't go back to fucking my then-girlfriend. So, for forty years, I've been sucking cock and fucking ass. I still prefer guys my age, but most of my fuckbuddies are too busy having sex with guys young enough to be their grandsons. I find that too pervy. Besides, I'm an economics professor and I can't afford the possibility of getting caught fucking a student. It's gotten way too easy for a student to accuse a teacher of sexual harassment if he doesn't get the grade he wants. Luckily, everyone knows I'm a hard-ass. It's a good reputation to have—anytime a kid accuses me of handing out too low a grade, one look at the rest of his semester's grades shows what a crybaby he is. It's happened to me twice, but on both counts, I was in the right. Even the parents called to thank me for standing my ground. They admitted that their kids could be a bit arrogant.

The other night when I logged onto this website, a guy— practically a kid, for god's sake—IMed me hello. He was eighteen; his age was posted next to a shot of himself grinning like a blond banshee in front of a bathroom mirror. He looked like just another smug college student who'd coasted through high school without doing all of his homework. I was about to delete his *hello* so I could focus on a few emails when he typed, *i heard about u.*

What the fuck had he heard about me?

like what? I typed.

let's meet

Who the fuck did he think he was? I decided not to answer.

u don't like being called daddy, right?

Of course. I'd specified "no daddy chasers" in my profile. *you got that right now leave me alone boy*

i don't like it when older guys call me boy

thats because you dont know whats good for you plus youre too young for me

u just proved what everyone said about u on here

What the hell was he trying to do, taunt me? I didn't want any more of his game-playing. I'd wasted my time online trying to hook up for way too long. Still, I checked his profile. He was local—as in, my city. That's a rarity. Most of the IMs I get are from guys in places that require a plane ride. It's as if they use the Internet to say hello and disappear like the cockteasers that they are. *what do they say about me?*

lots of stuff like how u are a worldclass prick

who told you that?

lotta guys here say u won't date anyone younger than urself

I grunted.

not exactly true i date guys around my age

I stared at the screen for a moment and resumed typing. *what the fuck do you want?*

let's meet

why should i meet you if youre not answering my question???

meet me tmw nite at giorgios 6 pm i'm paying

With that he logged off.

The little fucker didn't even give me a chance to turn him down. I looked at his picture again. He was wearing a white undershirt. There was some saying in Spanish—or Portuguese—tattooed on the underside of his forearm. He had a nose ring. His blond hair was probably dyed. He looked Hispanic, maybe Brazilian. I couldn't tell; It was hard to judge with photographs taken with a cell phone. Maybe it was an old picture. Maybe he was older than eighteen. Either way, I wasn't interested in barely legal guys.

I couldn't sleep that night. It had been a long time since someone asked me out on a date. I've got a small stable of friends with benefits, but when they found young men going gaga over them, I didn't get much action. Then it was just me and my left hand. It sucks, but that's life. Also, it takes me a lot longer to shoot now. I used to shoot three or four times a day, easy.

Then after the AIDS crisis happened, guys my age started doing the relationship thing. I thought it ridiculous. Why did they want to emasculate themselves by emulating straight folks? Men were designed to spill their seed as often as possible. I preferred to live alone with my cat and my books. Sometimes

I light up a cigar and let its smoke drift through my house. I'm up front about this in my profile: if you don't like cigar smoke, stay away.

So who did this eighteen-year-old fuckwad think he was? He didn't look like one of my students. But he had to know people on campus. I knew that when students registered for classes they compared notes, evaluating the propensity of professors to give easy grades. Most students took my course in world economics because they couldn't get into the more popular classes. I'd have liked to have been a popular teacher, but it seemed that the older I got, the more students were slacking off with their studies. Someone had to give them a whack. My students hated me every time they showed up in class: a single absence cost them twenty-five percent of their grades. I didn't care. Learning wasn't supposed to be a popularity contest. And I knew I was on the right track when a few students returned after a semester or two away to tell me, "I learned more from you than anyone else here." Students who pass my courses are the ones who do me proud.

I debated not showing up at Giorgio's. It's an upscale Italian restaurant that specializes in local and organic produce, not too far from my house. I had been there a few times, and it's certainly not cheap. I was intrigued: an eighteen-year-old kid was asking me out to an expensive restaurant on his own dime? What the fuck was he trying to prove? Was he a hustler trying to scam me?

I checked my profile. Why had he singled me out?

I'm wearing glasses without style in my profile picture, and my salt-and-pepper beard is bushy, the better to hide my chin, which is practically nonexistent. The beard gives the lower half of my face some definition. People say I look good, so that's good enough for me. I'm content to look like the academic I am, instead of trying to pretend I'm some kind of youngish stud-muffin. There are plenty of those out there. I've got a bald pate that shines in the sun and, in Internet parlance, I'm six-three, two-hundred twenty, hairy chested and average, as in *never work out.*

I waltzed into Giorgio's at six p.m., wearing a starched white shirt with a navy blue bow tie, pressed slacks and a tweed jacket. He needed to see that I was no spring chicken. He had to see that I was every inch a geezer so he could leave me alone. The restaurant was almost empty; the usual evening crowd hadn't flowed in yet. The kid was sitting by the bar, drinking a glass of wine. To my surprise, he wasn't wearing an embarrassing T-shirt-and-shorts getup: he sported a pin-striped suit with a vest and pocket watch and his black hair, no longer blond, was combed back, held in place by shiny mousse. No nose ring, either. He looked like a suave Italian from Francis Ford Coppola's *Godfather* movies—except that he was clearly Hispanic. When he turned and saw me, he stood with an extended hand. "Professor Devane?"

"Yes." I shook his hand and noticed his well-manicured nails. "I'm afraid I don't know your name—"

"Rico Martinez."

"Nice to meet you, Mr. Martinez."

He beamed, and then nodded to the bartender.

I turned to the front door. A waiter had posted a sign: CLOSED FOR PRIVATE PARTY. I turned back. "What's going on?"

"Dr. Devane, if you will." The young man held up his hand and beckoned forth the wine list. "Everything's on me tonight." I barely noticed the waiter. The light from above seemed to turn the menu in my hand white-hot. I squinted just to read the text.

"Whatever it is you're doing, stop right now. Please."

"Why? Am I scaring you, Dr. Devane?"

"No. I don't know what you want from me."

"You."

"Me? This old bag of a man?"

He broke into a grin. He had perfect teeth. Not a crooked incisor in sight.

"What's so funny?"

"You sure you don't remember me?"

"I teach many students. Year in, year out. I'm afraid you'll have to refresh my memory. You don't look eighteen."

"I'm twenty-five now. Seven years ago you told me that I wasn't fit for your class."

"You're not the only student I've said that to."

"When you said that, it really hurt. You had no idea."

I knew I should say something obligatory like, "I'm sorry." But I still didn't recognize him.

"I hated you. I hated everything about you. I hated the fact that I was letting a white older man tell me how I should feel about myself."

"I would've been fine with you thinking of me as just another privileged white male asshole to knock in your quest for racial equality."

He quietly smiled. "That's the papi I'd fallen for."

"Come again?"

"I've cum many, many times over you." He glanced around before he discreetly gestured jacking off.

I was embarrassed. "I'm sorry, but I still don't remember you."

"Seven years ago I was in your class. It was the third week. I showed up stoned out of my mind. I giggled at everything you said. You threw me out with the line I'll never forget: *You're not fit for my class.* You wanna know why I had to get high before

I went in your class? I was in love with you. I couldn't just sit there at my desk and drool. Hell, I jacked off over you three times a day. Usually more. I wanted you so much."

"But why me? You're handsome. You should stick to guys your age. Make your life easier."

"No," he said softly. "You were what I really needed in my life."

"This is making me feel mighty uncomfortable."

"Dr. Devane, you changed my life for the better."

"How?"

"That's why we're having dinner."

And he recounted the story of his young life. His father was an abusive drunk; his mother, a druggie. His aunts rotated their care of him. Once he graduated from high school, he met a wealthy older man and became a kept boy. But he wasn't happy with how the man treated him, or made drugs so readily available. Still, he paid for the teenager's tuition. He enrolled and showed up in my class. He really liked how strict I was. No one had truly stood up to him, and that scared him more than anything. When he left my class that day, he decided to quit college altogether. No one stopped him from spiraling down even deeper into a morass of drugs and promiscuity. Then he caught sight of himself, scraggly and zonked out, in a store window, scaring himself into blubbering his story to his first AA group. They listened. They took him to a treatment center. It took a while, but he sobered up, realized he wasn't an alcoholic and now had an occasional glass of wine with dinner.

By then his older lover had come down with pancreatic cancer. Tricks looted his house and disappeared. Rico was the only one who stayed with him through chemotherapy. They never discussed money, so he was surprised to learn, when the old man died, that he had willed him his entire estate. He paid someone to tutor him in how to carry himself better, how to shop for better clothes and how to appreciate the finer things in life. He enrolled in a university downstate and earned his degree in business administration and accounting. He invested his legacy wisely and was soon much more wealthy than even the old man had been. He now considered himself a fiscal conservative when it came to managing his own money.

"Seems you've learned something from my course. Good for you. So why are you telling me all this?"

"I never got the one thing that I always wanted, so when you gave it to this one girl in your class, I was so jealous. You just about killed me."

"Just what did I give her?"

"You were so proud of her when you handed back her paper. She had the only A in the class. When I saw that look on your face, I knew what I was missing from my life. I've never had anyone proud of me."

What could I say? I was overcome with emotion. I tried to find words, but I was speechless.

"You don't have to say anything," the young man murmured.

"No," I finally said, "I must. I still don't remember you, but I'm very proud of you. You knew what needed to be done, and you did it even if it wasn't the easiest road to take. That's what makes you a man." I placed my hand on top of his and gave it a slight squeeze. "A real man."

He looked at my hand, disbelieving, and turned to me with wide eyes. I chuckled.

"Seriously, you were the only reason I decided I had to do better. And seeing you tonight, I feel like a million bucks already."

"And then some."

He laughed. "Oh, you're funny. I forgot that about you."

I smiled.

He gripped my hand and kissed it. "I've wanted to do this from the first time I saw you."

I lifted his chin and didn't blink when I looked into his brown eyes. "Let's fuck."

Fifteen minutes later he was inside my foyer. His hands were all over me, but I gently set him back against the wall, next to the radiator. "Let me show you how proud I am of you." I knelt before him and fished out his cock, erect and uncut, its folds a work of art. I swallowed him whole without effort. He gasped loudly as my tongue flickered under the shaft right next to where his balls began. My fingers caressed the sensitive space between his thighs and balls. His cock leaked precum down my gullet.

"Daddy—sorry, I didn't mean to say that, sir."

I slowly took his cock out of his mouth and looked up at him. "My boy, you can call me anything. Call me Dad if you want. I don't care. I want to show you just how proud I am of you." I went back to his sweet sheath of skin and flesh. God, it had been so long since I tasted such thick foreskin!

"Dad, Dad, oh, papi!"

I reached around his ass and pulled him toward me. The fabric of his slacks felt incredible. There's something to be said for a high-quality weave.

He instinctively understood what I wanted.

He gripped the back of my head and thrust in and out of my mouth. His cock wasn't too long; in fact, it was just the right size. I could breathe through my nose and not take my mouth off his cock.

"Papi, I'm fucking your mouth, it feels so good...Uh-unh!" He tried to pull out. "Dad, I'm gonna blow..."

I looked up with my sternest professor look. "If you shoot

down my throat, you'll make me a very happy papi. Got that, boy?"

"Sí, papi." With that, he fucked my mouth with abandon. I kept up with him. "Papi, papi, papi…" His balls rose as I fondled them, my lips sealed tight. "Fuck fuck fuck!" he screamed as he volleyed thick gobs of semen down my throat. He didn't let go of my head as he quivered and deposited even more cum over my tongue. He sighed loudly when I licked cum from inside the folds of his foreskin and around his glans. I didn't swallow. He looked down at me with a far-off look.

I stood up. "What's wrong, my boy?"

"I can't explain."

I pulled him close and rubbed his back. It was strange to have someone sob in my arms. I didn't know what else I was feeling in that moment, but I was uncomfortable. I had spent my life fucking and sucking whomever I wanted, and I never had to hug anyone afterward. I've had a few guys express *feelings* for me, but I wasn't interested in dealing with lovey-dovey shit. But this boy—well, he was different. I had inspired him to change his life beyond textbooks. That was a novelty for me.

I kissed him on the forehead.

"Thank you, papi," he said. "You can fuck me if you want."

"Hey. You sound like a dejected student. I don't want to hear that kind of shit coming out of your mouth. From now on, if you want to be fucked, it's because you enjoy being fucked. If you don't like being fucked, it's fine too. You're not a kept boy. I can't afford you, and no, I don't want your money. If I want you, it's because you're a fucking hot boy with a killer smile."

He flashed his irresistible teeth and lit up.

"Such a hot boy." I took his face close to mine, and stuck out my tongue. He licked the remnants of his cum off and then fed it back to me.

"Open your mouth." I spat his cum back into his mouth. "Fuck."

I opened my mouth as wide as I could.

He spat his cum, diluted with our spit, back into my mouth. I swallowed, wrapped my arms around him and zeroed in on his luscious lips. Our tongues wrestled and our hands roamed. He had a gym-worthy body; the firm mounds of his pectorals had told me that much. Did he know just how fucking lucky I was to have him?

"Please."

I looked down to his fingers fumbling with the shirt buttons underneath my bow tie. "What?"

"I wanna see your chest."

I unsnapped my tie and unbuttoned to reveal my white undershirt.

"Fuck," he whispered as he caressed its fabric. "I always wanted to touch you like this."

"You can touch me anywhere you want, boy." I pulled the shirt off and pulled his face to my chest. "Suck your Daddy's tit."

He licked tentatively at first.

"You can nibble."

He bit almost too hard.

"Ow!"

"Sorry." He looked up at me with a great concern.

"Don't worry about it. You're doing great." Then I thought about what he wanted to hear the most, and said it: "Son." It was such a pervy thing to say, to my mind, but men don't always have control over what makes their cocks hard. Was it his fault that he was into the Daddy-son thing? He never had a proper father figure in his life.

He stopped licking my tit.

"Did I say something wrong?"

"No, no." He took off his suit jacket, pulled down his trousers and boxers, turned around and bent over. "Fuck me, Dad."

"You deserve better than just a fuck, son." I knelt and parted his lusciously smooth cheeks. He had the darkest hole of musk, and I licked all over its trench before I penetrated his puckered hole with my erect tongue. He groaned, appearing to be aroused beyond belief. I'd never felt so happy, teasing and torturing the voracious hole of the boy suddenly, surprisingly, in my life—because that's what he'd truly wanted. Sometimes you just have to give.

As he carried on in his near-incoherence, I unzipped myself.

"Lube's in my jacket."

I chuckled. "All right, son." I bent over and found a tiny vial of lube and a condom in a pocket. Both were high quality, of course. "Let me get this on."

"I can do that for you—"

"No. Next time. Later tonight. You're gonna shoot three times tonight."

"Oh, fuck fuck fuck." He writhed his hole at me.

My cock properly sheathed and lubed, I squirted lube all over his hole. "This feel good, boy?" I slipped in one finger, then another.

"Sí, sí. Fuck me now. ¡Por favor!"

I angled my cock downward, pulled his hips up and poised to push into his willing ass. I hadn't been this hard in years. "You okay, son?"

"Yes! Fuck me. Hard. I don't care. Just fuck me!"

"Just promise me one thing, son. Don't touch yourself. I wanna fuck you and fuck you and fuck you until you shoot."

"Oh, man...promise!"

There is an advantage to being older: it takes me a longer time to shoot than it used to, and I can fuck longer than younger tops who haven't learned the art of self-control. I gripped his hips and thrust in slowly, withdrew, thrust again, pushing the tip of my cock upward and downward and sideways, probing ever deeper.

"Fuck. You're so hard!"

"That's because you've made me so damn proud, boy." Then I rode his hole fast and ferociously. "If this cock could sing, it'd be chorusing praise for you to the world. There's no better boy than you."

"Oh," he moaned softly. "Thank you, papi."

"No need to thank me, son. You did all the hard work. I'm thanking you for making me so damn proud."

I continued thrusting, alternating slow with fast and staccato. My cock was right at home in his hole.

"Do your old man a favor, will ya?"

"What?"

"Think of your ass muscles like your fist. Squeeze and let go. Talk to me with your asshole, boy."

Instantly, it became a whole new mouth devouring my cock. Sometimes he squeezed hard when I rammed in; sometimes he didn't. He continued whispering in Spanish. I didn't know the language, but I resolved then and there that I would learn it for my boy. He'd gone through way too much on my behalf, and he deserved at least that much from me. He needed respect more than anything.

"Hey. You okay?"

"Yeah," he gasped. "I'm...I'm close, papi."

"How should I fuck you now?"

"Fast. Hard."

"You got it, son!"

He positioned himself firmly against the wall as I showed his hole no mercy. Miraculously, he was able to time the clenching of his sphincter with my thrusts. We were truly one, communicating in the most intimate language of all, and it had no words. He was telling me how much he needed me inside him, and I was telling him how much I needed to be inside him. No translation needed. I rammed and bammed against his hole, and his cheeks, though muscular, jostled from my thrusts. I slapped his butt.

"DADDDDDDDD!!!" he grunted. His body shook helplessly.

I leaned forward and grabbed him from behind. He was a rag doll flopping in my arms, still impaled on my cock.

"Fuck," he gasped at last. "That was the best fuck of my life."

"Good. But I'm not done yet." I guided him back against the wall. "You have to shoot one more time."

"Dad, can I suck your cock? *¿Por favor?*"

"You sure?"

"Yes."

I reluctantly withdrew and pulled the condom off my cock. It flopped upward against my belly.

"Wow," he said as he went down to his knees. "I didn't think your cock would be this beautiful."

"It'd feel more beautiful in your mouth, boy."

He slurped so enthusiastically and noisily, tugging at my balls and teasing my hole with just his dry fingertips, that I grabbed the back of his head. "Don't move, son." He held himself still as I bucketed a piston of sperm into his mouth. It had been a long time since I had cum so much all at once. My cum dribbled out the corners of his mouth.

Fuck, so hot, I thought. I pulled him up and opened my mouth. "Son, feed me your old man's cum."

He leaned close to my face.

The pearly whiteness of my cum coated his tongue. I couldn't believe that it was that thick!

I opened my mouth even wider.

He spit my cum to the back of my throat.

I pulled his mouth closer and kissed him. He reciprocated. We couldn't stop. I encouraged his hands to explore my body, and then I sucked his fingers while staring into his eyes. He looked like he was in heaven.

"Wanna make your Daddy real proud? Fuck him and show him what a man you are."

His voice cracked. "Really? You want me to fuck you?"

"Of course. But first I'm gonna get you nice and hard." I gave him a quick kiss on the lips before I slid down to my knees and took his semihard cock into my mouth.

"Wait, wait."

"Why?"

"I have to go pee."

"So?" I encircled the tip of his cock gently and brought my hands upward to his pectorals. I slowly rubbed the muscle of his chest in circular motions.

"Fuck fuck fuck," he whispered. He struggled to stay soft enough to pee.

I slowed the pace of my hands and he slowed his breathing. His eyes were closed. I stopped moving altogether, my mouth steady around the tip of his cock.

Finally, after what seemed like forever, his piss warmed my mouth and throat, a tentative trickle at first, before he let go a flood of golden nectar. I didn't lose a single drop. My boy needed to know how special he was.

He pulled out his limp cock. "You okay, son?" I asked.

"Fuck. That was like the greatest feeling in the world."

"Good! I still want to make you cum a third time."

"Are you for real?"

"I told you I wanted to make you proud, right? It's your turn to make me proud."

I returned to his cock, which plumped up nicely in almost no time. Ah, the joys of youth!

He babbled about how hot it was to let go of his piss like that, how he'd never done that before, how he'd seen online clips of guys doing that, how he was too afraid to ask to try it—

"Stop right there, young Mr. Martinez. Don't ever think that I'll judge you differently because of your kinky fantasies. In fact, I'll probably indulge the ones you know and teach you more!"

"Yes, Dad. Thank you, Dad."

"Good!" I resumed sucking his cock, but he pulled away. "What?"

"I wanna eat out your hole."

"Thought you'd never ask!"

I took his place against the wall. I wasn't prepared for the intense assault. There was no foreplay; he was all tongue-in-asshole. If his fast and furious rimming was any indication of his thrusting style, he was gonna ride my ass hard. It was going to be so easy for me to open up my hole for him; I had had forty years of all sorts of cocks and toys pushed up my back door. Rico gasped at how responsive my ass was to his lips.

"Go ahead and fuck me. It's your birthright." I listened to the crinkle of a condom wrapper being torn open. I turned to see his glistening erection, straining inside the thin rubber. I lathered lube over his cock as I kissed my beautiful boy, and then I took one of his hands and turned his palm upright. I spat. "Rub your Daddy's spit into my hole and breed me." I spread my legs and planted my hands against the wall.

His fingertips clutched my hip bones. Before I knew it, he

was all the way in. The bristle of his pubes scratched my ass. I flexed butt muscles around his rod. "Oh, yeah. Go ahead and breed your Daddy like a bitch."

"Oh, papi," he grunted. "*Te amo.*"

I balanced myself against him with one hand on the wall. With the other, I grabbed one of his hands from my hip and laved it with kisses. "You're my boy, my beautiful, handsome boy," I whispered.

As he fucked me, I felt the quivers tremble from his hands. I imagined him thinking about all the times he'd jacked over me, how long he'd waited for this moment. He was a sweet, sweet fucker. Usually, when a top fucks me, there's nothing but a cock in an ass, nothing genuine, no connection. Who'd have thought a twenty-five-year-old youth could make me feel this way? He was quiet, but his cock spoke volumes. It was telling me how much it had wanted me, how many years had passed since he first saw me in the lecture hall, how much he needed me. His swelling cock was as hot as a poker, ramming me furiously, seeking the fire exit. He was burning. I clamped down hard on his cock. "*Fuck me harder, son! Harder!*" I suddenly relaxed my ass muscles.

The sweet sensation of cum jetting against the condom's tip reverberated against my prostate. *Wow! That hasn't happened since I stopped barebacking back in the eighties.* I wasn't completely hard yet—he had cum too quickly. But I didn't care...after all, he was thirty-five years younger than me.

He collapsed forward and snaked his arms around me as he spasmed deeper inside me. I tightened my asslips again. I didn't want to let him go.

I took one of his hands and stroked my beard against it.

When his breathing returned to normal, I said, "You know something?"

"What?"

"You've taught me a great lesson tonight. I never cared for younger men, but I think you'll make an exceptional teacher."

"Me?" He pulled out, his soft cock flopping against my lower back.

I turned around. "Yes, you."

He looked at me curiously.

"You've taught me about what being a Daddy—something that once repulsed me—means. Tonight showed me how much I can learn from my boy." I unrolled the condom off his cock and pushed it inside out. "And I need to eat his cum for homework." I licked precious pearls off the latex. "Now, that's a real midnight snack."

He laughed.

Our clothes were strewn all over the foyer. I pointed to his shirt. "Take that off. I think your Dad's gonna like what he sees underneath."

His nipples look like perfectly melted Hershey's kisses.

"How about we go upstairs and shower?"

"Show me the way, and I'm yours." He pointed to the stairs. "Professor Papi?"

"How do you say *son* in Spanish?"

"*Hijo*."

I took his hand and beamed. "Let's go, my hijo."

IT'S MY JOB

Xan West

It's my job to stand still and take it for Daddy. I don't have to like it. I just have to stay standing, relatively still, and take whatever he wants to dish out. That's what boys do, he says, that's how you build a boy up. His job is to teach me how to be a man. Just like my job is to stand still and take it for Daddy.

Tonight he told me to lay out his leather. It's my job to take care of Daddy's gear. I know every piece intimately. He's wearing the chaps I just cleaned yesterday. His large furry belly hangs over them and my cheek aches to rub against it. The buttery leather is comfort to me, as much Daddy as his breath on my skin.

The belt he's wearing was passed from one man in his family to the next, on down to him. It is old and strong, and it has drawn my blood. When I hold it in my hands, it radiates with his strength. He has told me that when I am ready he will pass it to me.

The leather jock he wears was a gift from his Daddy. It has taken on his scent. Even after I clean it, it still smells of him, of musk and fur. The gloves he is wearing know my skin well. They are molded to his hands, a gift from his first boy, who made them specifically for him. My body is attuned to them. They graze my cheek and my lips automatically part, already tasting a mix of leather and Daddy so precious I just want to open myself up to worship.

And his boots. Oh, his boots. Corcs, they're a gift from his leather brother. Every boy that Daddy has taken in, from stray to slave, has fed these boots, with tears, fear, saliva and cum. Daddy's boots are magic. Home is Daddy's boots: Cleaning them. Conditioning them. Polishing them until they gleam. Walking behind them, my attention focused on being exactly at his heel. Sitting on the floor before them. Resting my cheek on them. Writhing on the floor under them. Being kicked by them. Feeding them. When I am attending to Daddy's boots, I know who I am.

He radiates purpose as he walks toward me in those boots, and suddenly I can't breathe. One hand grasps my throat and the other holds my chin. My lips part, my eyes widen.

"You going to be good for me, boy?"

His hand leaves my throat. I can think again.

"Yes, Daddy."

His hand is so fast I am caught off guard by the slap to my face.

"You going to stay still for Daddy?"

Slap.

"Yes, Daddy."

He slaps me repeatedly, his eyes holding mine as he talks.

"Make me proud, cub. Show me how strong you can be. A good boy can take anything and stay on his feet. I know you can do this for me."

I have stopped breathing. I am mesmerized by him.

"It's your job to stand still and take it for Daddy."

He slaps me once more and pauses.

"Yes, Daddy," I say, my voice trembling.

He kicks my feet apart and slams me into the wall. His weight feels so good. He slams me again, harder, thrusting my breath out. It feels so safe here, pressed up against the wall by Daddy.

The pain is not important. It is just a way to illuminate the path. It's important that my pain brings him joy. I sense it filling him as he begins to punch my pecs. He is radiating gladness, and I soak it in with every thrust of pain. There is something about the intensity of getting punched so near my heart, right by my throat and face, that makes me cry every time.

"That's it, boy," he says. "Cry for me."

He is relentless, driving into me, pushing me. The tears are flowing down my face. He pauses to lick them from my cheeks, wrapping his hand over my nose and mouth, taking my breath and filling my senses with leather.

"Good boy. Feed Daddy your tears," he growls.

Then he lets me breathe. He pulls on his SAP gloves, and the lead shot drives into me, challenging me to remain still for him. He smells different when he's hurting me, cold steel wrapped in Daddy-soaked leather. I breathe in, filling my nose with him, knowing it will make my heart race. The pain wraps around me, holding me close and warm.

Daddy turns me around and begins to kick me. My ass and thighs are on fire. I breathe in pain, exhale fear, and push my boots into the ground. It's my job to stand still and take it. I narrow my focus, concentrating on linking the soles of my boots to the floor with every blow. I can do this. I want him to be proud of me. As his boots connect with my thighs, I focus on riding the energy through my boots into the ground. I will please him.

He pulls out his police slap and begins to pound it into my

thighs like a sledgehammer, the lead shot ramming into me. It pounds me hard, and my dick begins to throb. He's hitting that spot where it starts to translate to sex. I am not a masochist, and there are very few intense sensations that feel like anything but pain. It is pure sex. My lips part, and I start groaning. It is all I can do not to bend over and beg him to fuck me now. I take each blow into my cock, feeling it swell until it seems like it's going to burst.

"You like that, don't you, boy? You like getting your ass pounded like a good little faggot. You wish my dick was in your ass right now, don't you, boy? This isn't about you. This is about getting me off, so don't expect I'm going to pay any attention to that hardening cock of yours, boy. The only dick you should be concerned with is this one."

He rams his dick against my ass, pushing my face into the wall, his hand on the back of my neck, holding it still.

"This dick is the one you should be focused on, boy."

He pulls back and picks up his favorite cat. It slams into my back, and I am utterly still: no breath; no movement. He begins to lay into me. The rhythm is hypnotic; fire dances along my skin as the cat drives into me. The cowhide is thin and braided, and the knotted tips feel like they are slicing me open. Waves of reddish-orange pain wash over my vision. My feet are planted. I will not move. I am helpless against the pain, lightning so strong it almost knocks me over. I am so small in the face of it. Nothing I can do will stop it. I stand still and take it, and it transforms me. I am taking it for Daddy.

I register a shift and know he has taken up his quirt. It is dedicated to me. It has drawn my blood and it will tonight. I gladly give myself to Daddy, tears, cum, fear, blood and all. The first wound opens and I hear his growl as he continues to slice me with two thin strips of leather.

"Everything you have is mine. I made you and I will hurt you, bleed you, eat you and fuck you as I please. That's it, boy. Bleed for Daddy."

We share blood, Daddy and I. In that way, we make real the relationship we have created. The intensity of that sharing is what wraps around my neck and connects me to him. It is the deepest sense of belonging I know, to be Daddy's boy, to feed him in all of his hungers. It takes everything within me to stay still for Daddy as he lays down his quirt and starts licking along my skin, drinking me in with his delicious mouth. I hold my breath with the effort, almost trembling with gladness. I can hear his boots on the floor as he walks away.

"Belly on the floor. Get your mouth over here, boy."

It's my job to use my mouth to please Daddy. I crawl on my belly toward him. He is sitting in his favorite chair.

"Get your mouth on my boot, boy. Show me some appreciation for all the attention you are getting tonight."

I breathe in the scent of his boot and begin to lick. Nothing tastes like Daddy's boots. Electric power fills them, and it surges through me as I worship. I can't help writhing at the feel of it. This is my place. I belong on the floor at Daddy's feet, my mouth on his boot. I know exactly what my job is, and that keeps me grounded.

All of me is centered around his boot: the texture of the leather; the taste of the polish and saddle soap, with undertones of piss and cum and tears worked in over the years. I savor it all with every stroke of my tongue.

"That's it, boy. It's your job to use your mouth to please Daddy. Show me how much you want to please me. Make me feel your mouth, boy."

His other boot comes to rest on the back of my neck, driving my mouth into his boot, making me writhe, my cock pulsing as it rubs against the floor. Daddy groans as I press my mouth onto the toe, taking it in like a cock, sucking on it. His other boot forces me onto it in a rhythm of his choosing, as I strain to take him in.

"Your mouth feels so good, boy. Now pay some attention to the other one."

I lunge for the other boot, taking the toe into my mouth immediately, my cock thrusting into the floor as I work my mouth onto it. The first boot slides between my legs and drives into my balls.

"The only dick that matters here is mine, boy. Daddy's dick is the one to focus on."

He grinds his boot deeper into my balls until the pain is too much and I begin to cry. He chuckles as he rams his boot between my legs harder. Tears drip onto the boot in my mouth.

"Good boy. Feed my boot with your tears. Now I need to feel your mouth on my leathers."

I lift my head to meet his eyes, surprised. He has never let me do that before, though I have dreamed about it.

"Yes, that's right, boy. You are going to lick your way up to the only cock that matters. Daddy's cock. Start with my chaps. It's your job to please Daddy with your mouth, boy. If you do, you just might get to taste Daddy's dick tonight."

I begin to lick, savoring the feel of the buttery leather on my lips. My eyes close and I breathe in the scent of it. Daddy begins to speak in a slow deep soothing voice.

"You did very well tonight, boy. You stood still for Daddy. You took everything I had. You fed Daddy right. You have earned the honor of worshipping my leathers."

My sole purpose in life is to please Daddy with my mouth. I open my mouth wider, licking intently along the leather of his chaps. My head between his calves, I writhe on the floor, intent on savoring every inch. I lick up to the knee on one and then switch legs, worshipping with luxurious strokes of my tongue. I can feel myself flying, airy. It is trancelike, and yet I'm completely focused. He groans when my mouth reaches the back of his knee, and his other leg clamps down onto my head, holding my mouth there as I continue to stroke him with my tongue.

"That's Daddy's good boy. Use that tongue. Make Daddy happy. Your mouth feels so damn good, boy."

His leg releases me, and I continue my journey up his thighs. Muscle shifts in response to my tongue. His hand snakes down and grips my hair before stroking my head. My cheek is against his leather jock. I can smell him. I am in heaven.

"Such a good boy for Daddy. Such a sweet mouth, so eager, so open for me. That's my good boy. Get your mouth over here."

He pulls my mouth onto his jock. I almost cum, right there. His boot slides between my thighs and the heel grinds into my cock. Tears well up in my eyes. His hand again grips my hair tightly, pulling it as he drives his boot heel into my cock, harder. I whimper, and tears fall onto his jock. He grips my head, rubbing my eyes into the jock to soak up the tears.

"That's right, boy. Cry for me. Cry on my cock. That's my good boy. That's what Daddy needs. Your tears. Be a good boy for Daddy and cry onto his dick. Daddy's dick is the only one that matters, isn't that right, boy? The only dick in the world is the one you are crying on, boy. Daddy's dick. Do you want to taste it, boy? You better lick that jock real good if you want to feel Daddy's dick in your mouth."

I move my mouth eagerly. I breathe in, savoring the scent and taste of Daddy. My whole being becomes centered on this small piece of cowhide separating me from Daddy's dick.

It's my job to please Daddy with my mouth. I will succeed. I ignore my dick. The only thing that matters is pleasing Daddy with my mouth. I am in the zone now. Nothing will distract me. Daddy's hand strokes my hair. I hear his growling groans faintly as I work my mouth on his jock. My focus is so intent that I start to whimper when his hand grips my hair, pulling my head back. I blink open my eyes and as my vision clears, I see it: Daddy's dick.

"Do you want it, cub?"

"Yes, Daddy. Please, Daddy. Please let me suck your cock."

"You have earned it, boy. You may suck my dick."

I eagerly move my mouth to him and take my time, licking around the head, taking it into my mouth to suckle, wiggling my tongue into the slit. I lick my way up to his balls and take them into my mouth, laving them with my tongue, sucking on them, gently running my teeth along them, breathing in the musky scent of Daddy.

"You do a good job pleasing Daddy, and you just might get a reward, boy."

I lick my way along the shaft, coating it with my spit, and then I start taking Daddy into me. I moan as I thrust my lips onto him. My eyes lift to his, and I begin to take him down my throat. All I care about is sucking him, for as long as he will let me, with as much skill as I can muster. He is hitting the back of my throat, and I struggle to take him down, gagging a bit, my eyes tearing, and then he's there—deep inside my throat, my nose in his fur. I swallow around him, rippling my throat on his cock. I could stay like this forever, my mouth locked on Daddy's dick.

It's my job to please Daddy with my mouth, and I can tell he is pleased as I look up at him. His eyes are locked on mine, and he reaches down to grip my head. Now I'm free; free to give myself over to his will as he rams into my throat, holding me still for his dick. He fucks my face so hard I am gagging, tears are streaming, and he does not stop or even acknowledge my struggle to take him in, just jams himself deeper. His eyes are feral. I am not breathing. I am not thinking. I am just a hole for Daddy to fuck. I am pliant in his hands as he moves my head, ramming me onto his dick.

"That's my boy. Daddy needs to use your mouth now. Take it for Daddy. Take my dick in your hole. Such a good hole for Daddy. That's all you are. A hole for Daddy's dick. Daddy made you and now he gets to use you. Use you up and eat you. That's what you are. Food for Daddy. Yes, boy. Those tears are feeding Daddy's leather. Let them fall. Such a good hole for Daddy. That's your only purpose right now."

He lifts my head to let me breathe just as I begin to gray out. He yanks me up and bends me over the arm of his chair.

It's my job to bend over quietly and take Daddy's dick. His hand on the back of my neck centers me as he spreads my legs, puts on a condom and lubes up his cock. My head is right where Daddy sits, and the leather chair smells just like him. I am surrounded by Daddy and leather, but I am scared. I always struggle to take Daddy's dick in my ass. It's terrifying every time.

He impales me with his cock, deep in my hole. It hurts. I whimper.

"That's my good boy. I know you're scared. Just remember, it's your job to bend over quietly and take Daddy's dick."

It's too big. I can't do it. It's bigger with every second. I stop breathing. Daddy's cock always feels like this: too big, like I really am eleven and am getting raped by my father for the first time. I tremble and shake my head. I know I'm supposed to be quiet, but I can't. I'm scared. It's too big. I can't. I can't. I can't.

"No, Daddy. It hurts. It's too big, Daddy. I can't do it. Don't, Daddy. Please."

Daddy knows better than to listen. He fucks me harder, his hand pressing my mouth into the leather.

"Shut up and take it, boy. It's your job to bend over quietly and take Daddy's dick, no matter how scared you are. No matter how much it hurts. You think this hurts, boy? I'm going to show you what hurting's really about."

There is no sound like a belt being ripped from its loops. It hits my back, on top of the marks from the quirt, breaking them open on the first blow. Fire races through me as he fucks me while his belt slams into my back. I am sobbing full out now, but I can't shut up.

"No, Daddy! Please, no. Please stop. Daddy, please! I'll be good. I promise."

"You will be quiet for me, boy. Until you figure out how to be quiet and take my dick, I will keep beating you bloody."

Daddy's dick slams into my hole. I can't breathe, it's so big. My eyes bulge, but my teeth clamp shut as he beats me. My screams are muffled by my closed mouth. He's tearing me open. I am shuddering. My entire body shakes as he pounds his belt into my back. Finally I find my quiet, and the beating stops. His dick is still invasive, but I take it for Daddy. He knows it is going to scare me each time. Daddy likes that. He leans into me, ramming me, and growls in my ear. "I can smell your fear, boy. You belong to me. Let Daddy devour your fear. Feed off your tears, your fear and your blood. That's my boy. Your job is to bend over quietly and take Daddy's dick. Just be Daddy's good quiet little hole. Let Daddy in."

I start drifting, and his words drop into me like rain.

"Just focus on Daddy raping your ass. That's my good boy. Take Daddy's dick. Daddy's dick is the only one that matters, boy. Just stay quiet and take Daddy into your hole. That's my good, good boy. You are being so good for me, boy. I'm going to let you cum. You hear me? Daddy's going to fuck you, and lick the blood off your back, and when he's ready you're going to hold your breath until Daddy cums. You hold it for as long as you can without breathing, boy, and when you are ready to burst, you cum for Daddy. That's my good boy."

Daddy leans down and starts licking the blood off my back as he fucks me. He is growling, and his dick just keeps ramming into me. As I am focused on staying good and quiet for him and feeling his tongue soaking up my blood, something shifts in me. I let go. I stop fighting him. I can just focus on doing my job for him without struggling inside anymore. Right now my job is to take him into me, to be a good quiet hole for Daddy's cock. And there's grace in that. I have a place. I belong to Daddy. I have a job. I know how to please him. All I have to do is let go and do my job, and everything will follow from that.

"Mine," Daddy growls as he licks the blood from my skin. "My boy to fuck. My hole to use. Mine. You are mine to do with as I see fit. You belong to Daddy. This is your place, impaled on my cock. This is who you are. I made you and I get to say who you are, faggot. You will learn to love this, as any good cub would. I will teach you. That's what Daddies do for their boys. Teach them how to be men. You will be a good man when Daddy's through with you. For as long as it takes, Daddy will teach you. You will learn."

He resumes ramming into me, brutal and relentless. He thrusts in deep with each word. I spent much of my adult life searching for a Daddy like this. I am so grateful to this man for pushing me like this, for trusting me with his cruelty.

"You. Are. My. Boy. My. Hole. To. Use. Made. By. Me. For. My. Pleasure."

He grabs my head and wraps his hand around my mouth and nose as he fucks me. All I can smell is leather. I can't breathe.

Daddy keeps slamming his dick into me, and I start to tremble. No breath. My head is pounding. My dick throbs as I begin to think about it again, getting ready to obey Daddy's order. And then his cock starts to feel good. I moan against his hand and have less breath. My eyes bulge, and I start to struggle against his hand. I can't breathe. Oh, god, his dick feels so good. I am screaming in my head. My cock is ready to burst.

Then Daddy's teeth sink into my neck. Searing pain roars through me and I can't breathe or think, or do anything except take it. Take his dick in my ass. Take his teeth in my neck. Take his cum as it spurts into me. It all explodes inside me, rushing through me and out my cock in intense painful spurts of cum. And then Daddy's hand leaves my mouth and we breathe together.

"That's my good boy. I am very proud of you," Daddy murmurs, as he pulls me to him.

His arms surround me, hands stroking. I can hear his heartbeat and I let my eyes flutter shut. I am safe in his arms. I breathe in, smelling leather and Daddy and cum. I am home.

ABOUT THE AUTHORS

GAVIN ATLAS (gavinatlas.com) enjoys writing Daddy stories more than anything, and most of the stories in his collection, *The Boy Can't Help It: Sensual Stories of Young Bottoms*, are intergenerational fantasies. He lives in Houston with his boyfriend, John, and he enjoys hearing from readers.

DALE CHASE (dalechasestrokes.com) has written male erotica for more than a decade, with two story collections in print: *If The Spirit Moves You: Ghostly Gay Erotica* and *The Company He Keeps: Victorian Gentlemen's Erotica*. Her novella "Tender Mercies" appears in *History's Passions: Four Erotic Stories of Sex Before Stonewall*.

LANDON DIXON's writing credits include *Options, Beau, In Touch/Indulge, Men, Freshmen, [2], Mandate, Torso, Honcho*, and stories in the anthologies *Straight? Volume 2, Friction 7, Working Stiff, Sex by the Book, Nerdvana, Ultimate Gay Erotica 2005, 2007* and *2008* and *Best Gay Erotica 2009*.

JAMIE FREEMAN (jamiefreeman.net) lives and writes in a small town in North Florida. More of his erotic fiction can be found in *Daddies, Muscle Men, Beautiful Boys, Video Boys* and *Homo Thugs*. He has published a variety of genre fiction, including romance, science fiction and horror.

JACK FRITSCHER (JackFritscher.com) is founding San Francisco editor of *Drummer* magazine, where he first introduced the concept of daddies in a 1978 feature, "In Praise of Older Men," leading to special issues titled *Daddies*. Eighteen books include the award-winning *Gay San Francisco; Some Dance to Remember: A Memoir-Novel of San Francisco 1970-1982*; and his bio of his lover, *Robert Mapplethorpe: Assault with a Deadly Camera*.

DOUG HARRISON's (pumadoug@gmail.com) prose appears in his PhD thesis, patents, zines and twenty anthologies. He was active in San Francisco's leather scene and appears in erotic videos and photo shoots. Doug has two children and two grandchildren. He lives in Hawaii near the lava flows of Puna.

DAVID HOLLY (gaywriter.org) lives in Portland, Oregon. His books include *Delicious Darkness*, a darkly erotic collection of over-the-top gay fantasy stories. His stories have appeared in *Best Gay Romance, Best Gay Erotica, Beautiful Boys, Boy Crazy* and many other publications, and he can be seen on facebook.com/david.holly2.

KYLE LUKOFF is a writer and aspiring librarian living in Brooklyn, New York. He has been published in many anthologies, including *Gender Outlaws: The Next Generation, I Like It Like That: True Tales of Gay Male Desire* and *Girl Crazy: Coming Out Erotica*.

JEFF MANN has published two books of poetry, *Bones Washed with Wine* and *On the Tongue*; a collection of memoir and poetry, *Loving Mountains, Loving Men*; a book of essays, *Edge* and a volume of short fiction, *A History of Barbed Wire*, winner of a Lambda Literary Award.

DOMINIC SANTI (dominicsanti@yahoo.com) is a former technical editor turned rogue whose stories have appeared in many dozens of publications, including *Country Boys, Brief Encounters* and *Best Gay Erotica 2011*. Future plans include more dirty short stories and an even dirtier historical novel.

RANDY TURK is single and living in Missouri. "Professor Papi" is his first story.

XAN WEST (Xan_West@yahoo.com) is the pseudonym of a NYC BDSM/sex educator. Xan's story "First Time Since" won honorable mention for the 2008 NLA John Preston Short Fiction Award, and other work has been published in *Best S/M Erotica 2* and *3*, *Best Gay Erotica 2009*, *Daddies, Sextime, Biker Boys, Backdraft* and *Leathermen*.

MARK WILDYR (markwildyr.com) has published about fifty stories exploring developing sexual awareness in the magazines *Freshmen* and *Men*, and in anthologies from Alyson, Arsenal Pulp Press, Cleis, Companion, Green Candy, Haworth and STARbooks Press. His novels *Cut Hand* and *The Victor and the Vanquished* are now available.

ABOUT THE EDITOR

RICHARD LABONTÉ (tattyhill@gmail.com), when he's not skimming dozens of anthology submissions a month, or reviewing one hundred or so books a year, or turning turgid bureaucratic prose into comprehensible English, or coordinating the judging of the Lambda Literary Awards for 2010-2011, or crafting the best croutons ever at his weekend work in a recovery center kitchen, likes to startle deer as he walks terrier/schnauzer Zak (sometimes accompanied by his husband, Asa) in Bowen Island's temperate rainforest. In season, he also fills pails with blackberries and huckleberries. Yum.

More Gay Erotic Stories
from Richard Labonté

Muscle Men
Rock Hard Gay Erotica
Edited by Richard Labonté

Muscle Men is a celebration of the body beautiful, where men who look like Greek gods are worshipped for their outsized attributes. Editor Richard Labonté takes us into the erotic world of body builders and the men who desire them.
ISBN 978-1-57344-392-0 $14.95

Bears
Gay Erotic Stories
Edited by Richard Labonté

These uninhibited symbols of blue-collar butchness put all their larger-than-life attributes—hairy flesh, big bodies, and that other party-size accoutrement—to work in these close encounters of the furry kind.
ISBN 978-1-57344-321-0 $14.95

Country Boys
Wild Gay Erotica
Edited by Richard Labonté

Whether yielding to the rugged charms of that hunky ranger or skipping the farmer's daughter in favor of his accommodating son, the men of *Country Boys* unabashedly explore sizzling sex far from the city lights.
ISBN 978-1-57344-268-8 $14.95

Daddies
Gay Erotic Stories
Edited by Richard Labonté

Silver foxes. Men of a certain age. Guys with baritone voices who speak with the confidence that only maturity imparts. The characters in *Daddies* take you deep into the world of father figures and their admirers.
ISBN 978-1-57344-346-3 $14.95

Boy Crazy
Coming Out Erotica
Edited by Richard Labonté

From the never-been-kissed to the most popular twink in town, *Boy Crazy* is studded with explicit stories of red-hot hunks having steamy sex.
ISBN 978-1-57344-351-7 $14.95

Only the Best from Richard Labonté

"Literally orgasmic." —*HX Magazine*

Buy 4 books, Get 1 *FREE**

Best Gay Erotica 2011
Edited by Richard Labonté
Selected and introduced by Kevin Killian
ISBN 978-1-57344-424-8 $15.95

Best Gay Romance 2011
Edited by Richard Labonté
ISBN 978-1-57344-428-6 $14.95

Beautiful Boys
Edited by Richard Labonté
ISBN 978-1-57344-412-5 $14.95

Boys In Heat
Edited by Richard Labonté
ISBN 978-1-57344-317-3 $14.95

Best Gay Erotica 2010
Edited by Richard Labonté
Selected and introduced
by Blair Mastbaum
ISBN 978-1-57344-374-6 $15.95

Best Gay Romance 2010
Edited by Richard Labonté
ISBN 978-1-57344-377-7 $14.95

Best Gay Bondage Erotica
Edited by Richard Labonté
ISBN 978-1-57344-316-6 $14.95

Where the Boys Are
Edited by Richard Labonté
ISBN 978-1-57344-290-9 $14.95

* Free book of equal or lesser value. Shipping and applicable sales tax extra.
Cleis Press • (800) 780-2279 • orders@cleispress.com
www.cleispress.com

Get Under the Covers
With These Hunks

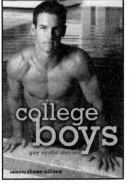

Ordering is easy! Call us toll free or fax us to place your MC/VISA order.
You can also mail the order form below with payment to:
Cleis Press, 2246 Sixth St., Berkeley, CA 94710.

ORDER FORM

QTY	TITLE	PRICE
_____	_____	_____
_____	_____	_____
_____	_____	_____
_____	_____	_____
_____	_____	_____
_____	_____	_____
_____	_____	_____
_____	_____	_____

	SUBTOTAL	_____
	SHIPPING	_____
	SALES TAX	_____
	TOTAL	_____

Add $3.95 postage/handling for the first book ordered and $1.00 for each additional book. Outside North America, please contact us for shipping rates. California residents add 9.75% sales tax. Payment in U.S. dollars only.

* Free book of equal or lesser value. Shipping and applicable sales tax extra.

Cleis Press • Phone: (800) 780-2279 • Fax: 510-845-8001
orders@cleispress.com • www.cleispress.com
You'll find more great books on our website

Follow us on Twitter @cleispress • Friend/fan us on Facebook